SOMET*there in* BETWEEN

S. FERGUSON

To Vicky
Always Remember
the something there
in between
S. Ferguson

Something There In Between

Copyright

Something There In Between

© S. Ferguson

1st Edition

Edited by Marla Esposito & Sue Banner

Cover Design by Shanoff Designs

Photographer: Wander Aguiar

Photographer: Victor Bezrukov

S. Ferguson

For Amanda

Thank you for helping me find me

Something There In Between

Table of Contents

Prologue

Bree

I hated that Ron had made me take a night off. I hated nights off. In the calm and silence, my mind was too much. I sat in the park for hours tonight just sitting on my bench. This had become my habit on my rare nights off, staring off into space. Sometimes, I cried. Sometimes, I just contemplated how it was possible to live through so much pain.
I always chain-smoked.

I didn't have it in me to walk to our… I mean *my* empty apartment. Some of his things were still there, taunting me that he's not coming back, reminding me that I am just another thing he left in an abandoned apartment, not caring enough to return for. Memories flash through my brain. They're burned into my head, and no amount of crying can purge them. Flashes of us.

Alex… saying he loved me.

Alex… teasing about how my bottom lip sometimes got caught on one of my front teeth when I was smiling really wide. Making out in whatever private place we could find, no agenda, just holding each other, and being together.

And, then, he was gone.

I take a shuddering breath, and look out into the nearly empty park. I was lucky that there was a small public park across from my apartment building; it was such an easy place to sit unnoticed for hours.

My heart is shattered. My life is in ruins. I run on autopilot: take a shower, go to work, and eat when I can't ignore the hunger anymore... everything I'm expected to do. I am living for the sake of living, but I am not alive.

Restlessness takes over my mind. I have to do something to distract myself. There is only one thing that can numb the pain, if only for a few hours. I'm not addicted to drugs or alcohol, but I am an addict. I pull out my phone, and browse through my messages, picking a few random guys I've hooked up with before. I know one of them will want to hook up. For an hour, I can pretend to be wanted. I can pretend I am beautiful. I can pretend my chest isn't a hollow, aching cavity.

Nate messages back quickly and, as usual, I head to his house for the customary booty call. I know he has a girlfriend, even though he tries to lie about it. He assumes I care. I have a few weak moments, where I wish I could be more than a fuck, but I know the score. I have no illusions. He doesn't know his girlfriend calls me about every other week anyway, asking me if I'm sleeping with him. I give her different answers, depending on my mood. She knows the score too; the difference between us is she's in denial. I know exactly what this is.

And I know exactly what I am.

Worthless. Unwanted. Slut.

I'm the girl you call for a fun time. You don't take me on a real date because why waste the money? You know you're going to get laid. You don't tell your friends about me; hell, you probably don't even tell me your real name. You lie to me about your girlfriend and, in some cases, your wife. The worst part is I know all of this. I smile when I know you're lying through your teeth. I nod when you tell me you want to fuck me. I smile when you lie, and tell me it's not just a hook up to you. But I know the truth.

I put up with your sloppy attempts to make romantic moves on me. Most of the time, I'm secretly rolling my eyes. I exist in a world of illusions. Some are stronger than others, but in the end it's all a lie.

Nate's routine is the same. He pretends to want to watch a movie with me, usually some foreign language film about Muay Thai. He makes a few attempted gropes at my chest, and then tries to enter me without a condom. He got away with it once, but now I'm onto his tricks.

When he finishes, I feel disgusted with myself. Nausea bubbles in my stomach, as he rolls over and starts to snore. He doesn't bother to say goodbye. I'm not the kind of girl that deserves the extra energy. I dress quietly and leave. I know he has roommates, but I've never seen any of them. Sometimes, I wonder if he does that intentionally. He's never taken me anywhere public, despite fucking me off and on for the last few months. I walk out onto the street in front of his building, and light up a cigarette. Flipping through my phone, I find some music and start the walk home. Well, back to my park. I sit there and cry, lighting cigarette after cigarette.

I will never be whole again.

How did this become my life?

Chapter 1

Declan
Present Day

"I was sleeping, asshole," I mutter, standing and stretching my long legs out. I really needed to get a bigger bed; this full size mattress barely has room for half of my six foot and five inches long frame. Unfortunately, the apartment I could afford barely has room for the bed. It's a vicious circle.

"Like I give a fuck…you still looking for a job?" Jake asks, as I hear him moving around, his voice lowering to almost a whisper. Knowing my brother and his whoring ways, he's probably trying to sneak out from wherever he crashed last night.

"Yeah, man, you got a lead?" I ask, making my way to my beloved coffee maker.

"Yeah, Boss needs another bartender," he says casually, as if his criminal mastermind of a boss hasn't needed another bartender for the last year…as if I haven't been asking about that same job for pretty much that entire year.

"Are you fucking serious? What changed? That girl quit?" I start my Keurig while trying to remember her name. It started with a B, I think. She has been there since my brother was a newbie, and the guys all seem to love her. She's also pretty hot, if I remember correctly, but she keeps to herself, and never runs her mouth about Ron's business. That makes her invaluable.

"Nah, she's still there. Her douchebag boyfriend was the one who took off. He still hasn't come back, and Boss was waiting to replace him out of respect for Bree, but she's getting overwhelmed, managing the bar and working every damn day. Plus, we got a couple big meetings coming up."

I immediately stop all movement. "What kind of meetings?"

There was always some wannabe criminal on the verge of a turf war with Ron, Jake's boss. My brother's experience working for Ron had been relatively peaceful but the few times things had taken a violent turn, it almost always started with some kind of "meeting."

"Yeah, Boss says Tony wants peace, which means lots of meetings and lots of parties. There's gonna be so much tail floating around. It's a win-win for you. Job makes bank, and more pussy than you'll know what to—" Jake's voice is abruptly cut off by a screeching noise.

"WHAT THE FUCK, JAKE?" I hear a woman shouting. I can't help but start laughing.

Jake getting busted for sneaking out of some random's apartment is highly entertaining to me. I'm a good brother like that. Fucking Jake and his inability to keep it in his pants. Fear of commitment would be an understatement. I understand his reasons, but I don't agree with them. I want nothing more than to find the girl for me, and create my own family. God owes me a do-over after the shit family he gave me the first time around.

"Fuck. I gotta bail. Come to the bar tonight, and Ron will hook you up. We need someone we can trust and you're family." Jake hangs up before I can respond.

I want to remind him I'm not family anymore, not really. Sure, we share blood but Jake's fellow thugs are his family now. When he decided to go work for Ron, he tried to talk me into joining with him, but I didn't like the idea of having to follow someone else's orders. I was done following someone else's whims. I know I probably should have some moral reason, but the truth was that a life of crime didn't bother me, not after everything I'd been through. But, if I was going to jail, I was going for myself, not someone else.

With a sigh, I set my phone down on the counter next to my abandoned coffee. Rubbing my hands down my face, I try to decide if this is really what I want. Not too long ago, this job seemed like the best thing that could ever happen to me. Now, I know enough about Ron and the bar to realize it could be the most dangerous thing that ever happened to me as well. No, I take that back. Nothing could be more dangerous than living with my dad. I survived that asshole. I'll survive this.

My mind flashes back to Jake as a scrawny kid, crying as I shoved him under my bed, trying to hide him from our father. I didn't always manage to hide him in time, but I always did my best. I've always been his big brother, his protector. Ron or not, this is my best chance to protect him, and to keep an eye on him.

It doesn't take me long to realize a run will clear my head. I usually run every morning, but had planned on sleeping in this morning. *Thanks for killing that, Jake.*

I brush my dark, shoulder length hair, and pull it into a ponytail at the base of my neck, before I slip on gym shorts and my favorite running shirt. It says, "World's Okayest Runner" and never fails to make me smile when I wear it. Stupid t-shirts are kind of my trademark, that and converse shoes. I have one pair of shit kicker boots and that's it. All my other 15 pairs of shoes are converse. It's been a real source of contention with my old girlfriends.

At least working at Ron's bar will probably mean no stupid uniforms. I know he and his guys wear suits most of the time, but the bar has always had a casual vibe. When I think about some of the dumb shit the other places I've bartended at have made me wear, I can't help but shudder.

Locking my apartment, I walk out onto the street and stretch while trying to decide how far I want to run. The fall weather is perfect for outdoor running. All too soon, I'll be stuck on a treadmill in my apartment's gym while the ground is covered in ice and snow. Considering that it's most likely gonna be a late night, starting the new job and bartending can be pretty physical, I decide to keep it at around 3 miles. I smile when I hit my stride and my head clears. Running always came easy to me, and helped balance out my complete lack of discipline with food. It's not long before my runner's high hits, and I completely space out, going into the zone.

When I'm cooled down, and finish stretching, my restlessness returns with a vengeance, and I don't want to go home and just sit in my apartment. I remember there's a park right around the corner, and decide I'll go hang out for a bit to enjoy the weather a little longer.

There's only one bench in the small park, and there's a young girl already sitting on it. I pause for a moment, trying to decide how creepy it would be to sit next to her, before deciding it's not worth stressing about. It's a public park, it's daytime and I'm not going to bother her. I make a wide arc, coming to the bench from the side instead of from behind, so she can see me approaching.

As I get closer, I realize she's not as young as I originally thought; she's definitely in her early twenties. She's also dressed in all black, except her shoes. She's wearing glitter-covered converse. It goes without saying she has my interest now. Her jeans are black, and look skin tight, with a few strategic rips in them, showing glimpses of firm thighs I would be more than willing to rub my face on. Her shirt is a mostly loose, black t-shirt that her small but perky breasts are pushing against. I steal a second glance to see if I can spot any nipple, and my cock perks up a little at the idea, but I quickly raise   my eyes. She has hair so black it's almost blue, loose and hanging over her shoulders in thick waves. She's sporting a sleeve tattoo on her left arm and it's hard to make it out from here, but it looks like a bunch of writing, which I find interesting. I always was a sucker for a girl with ink. I speed up the rest of my walk to the bench, and sit down on the opposite end.

She turns her head, and my eyes quickly look up from perusing her body. Holy fuck! This chick is gorgeous. Her eyes are a pale blue, almost the same color as the irises my mom always kept in the house. She's got them lined with that black shit that chicks love, and it only makes them seem brighter. What captures my attention about her eyes though, isn't just how beautiful they are, but how haunted they look. There is sadness in them that I've never seen in someone so young. This girl is defeated. I recognize that look immediately, after spending so many years seeing it every day on the face of someone I loved. A feeling of protectiveness rises in me. I want to grab her and hold her. Tell her everything will be okay. I give my head a mental shake, and continue taking in the rest of her face. Her lips are painted bright red. Some girls can't pull off the look, but she makes it look effortless. I won't lie, and say I'm not imagining those red lips sliding up and down my cock.

I shift my legs, trying to get comfortable and conceal my growing erection. I'm not a small guy, and my running shorts won't hide shit. I look back up at her, and am relieved that she seems to have missed my adjustment. Something about her seems familiar though, especially when I take in her all black clothes again and those shiny converse. Those shoes are killing me; they are obviously proof we're soulmates.

She has a small piercing in her nose, and her eyebrows are currently raised like I scared the shit out of her. Fuck, maybe she did catch my ill-timed boner.

"Sorry I didn't mean to scare you. I'm Dec, well, Declan but everyone calls me Dec." I'm fucking babbling. Jesus, what's wrong with me?

"You didn't scare me. I was just leaving anyway." She starts to rise, completely ignoring my attempt at an introduction.

"Look, don't run off just because I sat here, too. I can be quiet and let you enjoy the um…" I glance at the mostly brown grass and rusted out swing set. "The view."

The corner of her mouth turns up slightly into a smirk, and I mentally high-five myself for getting a reaction. I can already tell this is a chick that will make me work for anything I get.

"Can you really be quiet? I come here to think when I can't take…" She cuts herself off, and her cheeks get a tinge of pink.

She exhales sharply and continues, "When I get tired of sitting in the apartment."

I find something about the way she said that odd, but I can't quite figure out which part, and I immediately decide to let that go. Clearly, she's got something going on, sitting here in her all black outfit and shiny shoes… and that's when it hits me. I *know* her.

"Hey, you're the bartender, right? You work at Keegan's?" Odd name for a bar, I know, but Keegan was Ron's son. He died ten years ago, at 14, from cancer. Ron named the bar after him and, even though I think naming a bar after your kid is kind of odd, I don't judge Ron for it.

"I don't know, do I?" she asks, her face immediately turns to stone, and she meets my gaze dead on. I realize how bad this looks. A random guy approaches her on the bench, sits next to her, and starts asking her about the bar she works at, a bar anyone worth anything knows belongs to Ron.

"Hey, I'm not a cop or anything. My brother works for Ron. His name is Jake, and he's always hanging out with Greg." I spit out the name of my brother's best friend like it's a curse. It would be a complete lie for me to say I'm not jealous of their relationship. When Jake started working for Ron, Greg was assigned as his partner, and he quickly became my replacement. The two of them are always together; they even seemed to have their own secret language. If I didn't know Jake slept with basically every girl he met, I would have thought they were a couple or something.

Her face remains unreadable, but her eyes are smiling, when she stands. "I don't know a Jake or a Greg. Have a good one." She gives me a parting flick of her wrist. I think it was supposed to be a wave, but it definitely came off as more of a dismissal, and then she starts walking toward the apartment building across from the park.

That was definitely B Girl, the bartender Jake and I were talking about earlier. Ron owns that building, though few people know that. I'm sure Ron put her up in that when he hired her. He would want to be able to keep an eye on his employees, especially one that worked in the bar. It was a poorly kept secret that his office was in the back of Keegan's. I'm also pretty sure I remember Jake saying something about her being a runaway when she started working for Ron. I smile, watching her disappear as quickly as she can. Just like that, the decision to work for Ron is sealed. Little does she know, she's going to be seeing a lot more of me…starting tonight.

Chapter 2

Bree

After I've walked into my apartment, I shut the door and lean back against it, letting myself catch my breath. I smile at the coincidence of running into Jake's babbling brother as I wander into my kitchen for a drink of water. My mouth had instantly gone dry when Declan approached me.

I didn't miss the way he seemed to snarl Greg's name too. There was definitely some tension there. I'm going to have to think about that one for a bit. Jake and Greg are absolutely inseparable.

Jake's brother was very different from what I expected. Whenever Jake talked about him, he described Declan as serious and uptight, but that's definitely not the impression I got from him today. He was also really hot, if I'm being honest with myself, even in plain running clothes and covered in sweat. He had the whole bad boy thing going on with his long hair, scruff, and gauges in his ears. His funny t-shirt seemed like such a contradiction from the bad boy image. Considering I work around almost no one but your stereotypical bad boys, the fact that he stood out to me is significant. I could see he had some tattoos on his arms as well, but I didn't want to look too closely and seem like I was checking him out. His eyes were the most amazing part of him. I don't know if I've ever seen eyes that green. They reminded me of the moss you see growing deep in the forest, untouched by humans and the sun.

I'll have to take a closer look next time, I think, and I even catch myself feeling a little excited at the idea of seeing him again. Then a wave of sadness hits me, bringing me back to reality. It doesn't matter how hot I think he is, he's not going to be interested in me. Maybe, if I'm lucky, he'll want to do a quick hookup, but I'm not going to be what he wants in the long run. I am not capable of being that girl.

As if my heart needed an additional reminder, I look down and see Alex's shoes sitting on the floor by where I'm leaning against the front door. I'm probably crazy for not throwing his stuff out. I read on the Internet once about a girl who burned all her ex-boyfriend's stuff in a trash barrel when he left her. Call me crazy, but I like the reminder. I need to remember. I need to remember that I am damaged goods. There would be no happy ending for me. If I ever forgot that, I'd run the risk of being hurt again. Something I wasn't sure I could survive. I would never let myself be suckered into thinking I was loved again, because I knew better. With this reminder burning into my brain, I walk across the small studio apartment and curl up on my bed. The last things I see before I shut my tear-filled eyes are more of Alex's abandoned belongings. It creates a warped sense of balance that all of his abandoned things are in one place: his clothes, his shoes, me. We're all still here in purgatory.

****

After an all too short nap, I do a quick primp and finish getting ready for work. Ron had made it clear when he hired me that I wasn't expected to put out like the other girls tend to do, but I was expected to be somewhat sexy at work. I was seen as a representative of him, and that meant I had to look the part when I was serving his guests in the bar. That didn't mean I had to let my ass hang out. Originally, the biggest reason for our arguments was Alex; he was extremely jealous and hated the idea of me working at Keegan's with all the men checking me out. Unfortunately, there was nothing that could be done, and Ron did a great job of making it clear that I was off limits the few times a random idiot wanted to try anything.

I stayed dressed in my super tight black jeans; well, everything I owned was black to be honest. I found my solid black wardrobe discouraged people from approaching me. It was also the uniform for Keegan's. It made things easier for me. I traded my converse for my black ballet flats, the biggest concession I had gotten from Ron when arguing about my wardrobe. I couldn't walk in heels for shit. I grimace as I remember Alex's new girlfriend's long legs and her high-heeled boots. Just another reason why I wasn't good enough, I guess. I shake my head and put my tight t-shirt on; it has the bar's logo on the front right pocket, a large K done in white rolling script. The shirt's about two sizes too small, and makes my B cups look like D cups, especially with my pushup bra underneath. It's got a V-neck that also shows off my manufactured cleavage. I delicately run my fingers through my wavy hair, thankful for the natural body it has; that saves me a lot of time.

Deciding that I'm as ready as I'm going to get, I grab my green military jacket and lock up. I step out onto the street, and see the sun setting. Another day gone and nothing has changed. I still can't believe this is my life. It's both worse and better than I ever expected. I always feel like I freed myself from one trap just to walk right into another. I dismiss the pointless train of thought, make sure the building door shuts behind me, and take off.

I make a quick stop on the way to work at the corner store.

"Hey Bree, how's it going?" Stan, the owner asks from his perch on a stool behind the counter.

"Same as always," I mutter. If that isn't the truth I don't know what is.

"You should try smiling sometime, it could change your life." Stan says cheerfully.

"You need something to smile about first," I mutter, throwing a few dollars on the counter and walking out with my protein bar.

Something There In Between

S. Ferguson

Chapter 3

Declan

I'll totally admit that meeting B Girl made the decision to go work at Keegan's easier for me. Something about her calls to me. I've heard enough over the years to know she doesn't hook up with anyone, even after her boyfriend left. Challenge accepted, B Girl.

Once I return home from my run, I spend the rest of the day back in my apartment, doing meaningful things like playing video games and listening to music.

I take a quick shower to get ready for Keegan's and find myself thinking about B Girl again. This time things are a little naughtier. Those red lips of hers run through my mind over and over again.

Taking myself in hand, I run my hand from base to tip, slowing increasing the tightness of my grip. I groan loudly and drops of pre-come begin to form on the head of my dick.

Suddenly I'm not remembering B Girl on the bench anymore, I'm the one on the bench and she's kneeling in front of me. She's looking up at me, those beautiful blue eyes wide and those bright red lips parted as she takes me out of my jeans. Fuck.

It takes me an embarrassingly short time to come and I rinse myself off enjoying the temporary lack of tension in my body. It won't take long for my nervousness about working for Ron to come back.

I give myself a once over on the way out. Taking a cue from B Girl, I decide to replicate her all black look, except my Chuck All Stars are bright red. See, she's definitely my soulmate. Of course, my black t-shirt has a giant red Stormtrooper head on it. I had to put my signature somewhere.

The walk to the bar is quiet and quick; I hadn't realized how close I lived before. As I make my way inside, I pull my hair up in bun and look for Jake, but only see a handful of guys sitting around the scattered tables and chairs. I walk over toward the closest table.

"You guys seen Jake?" I ask, before I recognize Greg sitting at the table. For once, I'm grateful for running into him. If anyone will know where Jake is, it's him.

"Who's asking?" Greg sits back in his chair with an I-fucking-dare-you expression on his face. What an asshole.

My jaw ticks at his attitude. Greg knows damn well who I am. I've never been the type to take any shit, but this isn't the time or the place. I unclench my fists and walk towards him, extending my right hand. "I'm Dec, his brother. I'm supposed to come see Ro—-The Boss, about working behind the bar." I deserve a medal for not rolling my eyes. God, why do I feel like I'm in a bad mafia movie?

He looks at my hand like I have some sort of disease, and I quickly drop it back to my side. My fist clenches with the need to smack that look right off of his face.

"Does Bree know you're gonna be working with her? She's gonna fucking love that." He smirks, and the other guys at the table start chuckling. Could this guy *be* any more of a douche bag? Bree! That was B Girl's name. I make a mental note to still call her B Girl, I don't know why. I guess I have a love for antagonizing people. Okay, that's a lie. I totally know why. I want to get under her skin any way I can. I don't care how pissed off she is, as long as she's focused on me.

"Do I know what, Greg?" Bree asks, walking towards the table with what is clearly impeccable timing.

"That I'm your new best friend?" I quip, turning to look at her. Seeing her again takes my breath away just like it did the first time. I note with some disappointment she's traded her chucks for a pair of flat shoes. I quickly turn back to Greg, trying not to show my frustration about that fact that he's acting like he doesn't recognize me. Judging by the smirk he's been sporting since I walked over, I'm right in my assumption.

"Guess you really did know Jake," she says, her voice changing to an almost singsong tone. She's got sass, even if she tries to hide it sometimes.

"You know this clown?" Greg is giving me another once over, and there is nothing nice about it. Despite feeling like I'm being sized up by a predator, I give him an eye roll. He narrows his eyes at me, and I decide if I'm going to piss him off, why not go for gold?

"Didn't tell everyone about our park date?" I tease Bree, who is looking at me like I'm a piece of gum stuck to her shoe.

"Trust me. You don't want these guys thinking you stalked me to the park and tried to ask me about Ron's bar." She looks like she wants to smile, that same left corner of her mouth is lifted in a smirk. I get the feeling that if she ever gave me a full smile, my heart wouldn't be able to take it.

"This motherfucker did what?" Greg starts to rise from his chair. I take a step back, bracing myself to get my ass handed to me. I could probably handle Greg one on one, but we both know we're in his territory. No way are his friends not going to jump in.

"Bree, new kid, my office now," Ron calls from a door to the right of the bar, saving me from Greg's next move.

Greg's smirk turns into a smile I'm pretty sure the Devil himself has given a time or two before.

Bree takes a deep breath, and starts walking ahead of me. I decide to seize the chance to check out her ass. It's amazing by the way. I swear I hear a growl come from behind me, and I immediately raise my eyes to the back of her head. I smile to myself. *Challenge accepted.*

Ron's office isn't anything like how I would have expected a crime boss's office to look. The building is old, with a high ceiling, and I would say Ron took the building's age into account when he decorated his office. It looks more like an antique shop, with a mixture of carefully placed modern touches. There is a large oriental rug, giving the room a warm feeling, and mostly likely stopping any echoing. The real centerpiece of the room though, is a painting. The painting is of a little girl with jet-black hair dancing on the beach by herself. She's wearing a white, flowing summer dress, and looks like she is spinning in circles, her eyes closed, arms stretched wide, a peaceful smile on her face. I look at her face for a moment, and start to look away, before doing a double take. Surely, I can't be the first person to notice the similarity between the girl and …

"I know you don't want anyone else behind the bar. I know it was that fucker's job, but we all know he isn't coming back. Soon, we have one of the biggest meetings of the year coming up, and you can't handle that by yourself. Not to mention, if the shit hits the fan, you need someone to help keep you out of it." Ron says, cutting my thoughts off.

The faint odor of cigar is in the air, as I stop my perusal and Bree sits down in a chair across from Ron's desk.

While Ron talks, I get a good look at him for the first time in years. He rarely goes out and about anymore; too many people want a piece of him. He has people, like Jake, to run his errands. After Keegan died, he retreated from public life. There are rumors he has a daughter, but it's just that: rumors. If that little girl exists, she's a ghost. He looks older. Weary. His dark brown hair has more silver at the temples. His blue eyes have a tiredness in them that I know has nothing to do with needing sleep. Life has been hard on Ron, and it looks like it hasn't gotten any easier, even with his success.

Bree is sitting in complete silence. Her face is a mask of stone, and her posture is stiff. "You know I can take care of myself." Her tone is as stiff as she is.

"Darlin', you're one of the strongest people I know, but at the end of the day you're still five foot nothin' and a woman. We don't hit women, but I can't promise others won't. You need help. This is not up for negotiation. Declan will be working every shift with you from now on, so get used to it." He gives her a look I would almost describe as fatherly before he turns his attention to me.

Something There In Between

"You keep your fuckin' hands to yourself, listen to whatever the fuck she tells you, and don't give any shit to my boys. I know you're Jake's blood, and he trusts you, which means I trust you, but if you fuck me over, you'll both pay." He gives me a hard glare with none of the softness he just gave Bree. I nod my head because honestly, the guy is fucking terrifying. He reaches over to his phone, which hasn't stopped buzzing, and picks it up.

Apparently, this means we are done talking because Bree stands abruptly. "Come on," she mutters, almost too softly for me to hear, as she marches out of the office.

She spends the next three hours speaking to me only when absolutely necessary. There's a lot of grunting and pointing involved. To be honest, the whole situation is kind of amusing.

I find as many things as I can to keep myself busy, lifting the heavy racks of clean glasses and replacing a few empty kegs. I also spend a good amount of time studying the layout of the bar.

The bar faces the front doors, which are heavy and wooden. I'm sure they're as old as the building, which means they match the rustic décor, but I imagine they also serve a purpose for security. They're probably thick enough to be bulletproof, from the average gun anyway, and almost impossible to ram open. Ron's office is to the right of the bar and the rest of that side is all heavy wood paneling, with a few dartboards and three pool tables in a row. The other side of the bar is all brick. There is a kitchen with another exit behind the bar, but it's rarely used from what I understand. All the equipment is old, and covered in white cloth, to keep dust off. I also know there is a back door leading outside from Ron's office. Directly to the right, outside of the kitchen's backdoor, is a staircase that leads to apartments above the bar. From what Jake has told me, no one actually lives in them, but there is an understanding that those rooms can be used by Ron's guys if they need a place to crash or screw. There are also no windows, anywhere. I'm assuming this was done as a security measure, but I can't help but feel a little trapped. It's very apparent that no one is entering or leaving this bar without permission.

A few of the guys introduce themselves. For the most part, they're pretty welcoming when they find out I'm Jake's brother. It's a pleasant surprise to see that so many of the guys think so highly of Jake.

I watch Bree to see how she runs things, where things belong, but bartending isn't that different from place to place, so it doesn't take me long to get the hang of things. I never stop watching her, though. Few things in life are as fascinating as she is. I notice she bites her bottom lip when she's concentrating. She licks her lips when she does something strenuous. She is great at making mixed drinks, but when she pours a draught, she always has way too much foam on the top. No one says anything to her about it, though. She tries to do everything herself, but one of the guys always seems to magically appear if she's trying to reach something up high or lift something heavy. *That shit is gonna end now that I'm here,* I think to myself, feeling strangely possessive of Bree. I want to be the one who helps her, the one she turns to.

Usually, the first one to offer to help is a tall, skinny guy wearing dress pants and a stiff dress shirt with the top two buttons undone and the sleeves rolled up. He introduced himself as Quinn, and gave me a warning similar to Ron's about keeping my hands to myself. I completely ignored his warning. Ron may be someone to take seriously, but this guy is nobody. That being said, something about him doesn't quite sit right with me. His pupils tell me he's been consuming more than alcohol tonight, which is pretty interesting considering Ron's zero tolerance policy on drugs is pretty well known.

The night starts to calm down; most people are off sitting at the tables in small clusters talking. I try to remember everything I know about Bree, which isn't much. I'm pretty sure she was homeless, and some asshole brought her into the bar to try to trade her off as one of Ron's 'hospitality girls' (I'll let you figure out what that means) in exchange for food and shelter, but she was too young. Ron and his guys can be bastards, but they aren't child molesters. No way would Jake tolerate that shit after our childhood.

Ron clearly has a soft spot for her, and she's gotta have a good work ethic to have stayed here this long, especially by herself for the last year.

After a while, I figure out she really isn't going to smile. It seems odd to me that someone so young, granted I was only a few years older, could be so serious all the time. She moves quickly and efficiently, and she never wastes her energy. Bree clearly has had this job for a while and I was willing to bet she could do most of it with a blindfold on. She doesn't really talk to anyone. A few of the guys greet her, some of them try to chat, but it seemed like everyone knew not to bother her. That guy, Quinn, who I found out joined Ron's outfit shortly after my brother, seems to have a thing for her, planting himself at her end of the bar, and throwing back whiskey like his life depends on it, never taking his eyes off of her.

After watching her in a borderline obsessive way, it hits me: she's on autopilot. She may be alive, but she isn't living. *What happened to you?* I thought. What exactly had gone down in her life to make her homeless at 16, and what had happened with the ex? He was clearly on Ron's shit list, which is definitely not a good place to be. I can't help but think, *here's my chance.*

Chapter 4

Bree

I was relieved that Declan turned out to be who he said he was. I didn't want to have to tell Ron that someone had been nosing around me or his business. I knew I was only as valuable as my silence, and I didn't want to find out what would happen if that changed. It may seem kind of pathetic to still have the will to live, but despite everything, it was there.

Declan seemed determined to spend the majority of the night watching me. I mean, *really* watching me. It's unnerving. I knew he would want to pay attention to how I ran the bar, to see where everything went, but I felt like I was being studied. Memorized. Under his scrutiny, I found myself afraid of what he was seeing. I prided myself on remaining invisible. I never talked to anyone at the bar, except for Ron, beyond the necessary small talk. I never socialized with anyone outside of the bar, except for my hookups, if you wanted to call that socializing. I was afraid he would see me, really see me, something no one except Alex has done. The thought that Declan would see what a bitter disappointment I was, frightened me. I didn't know why. His opinion shouldn't matter to me. Besides, I can't be upset about someone seeing the truth, yet I grew more and more tense as the night wore on. Most of the guys were pretty good about leaving their impressions of me as being a pretty face, a reliable bartender, and someone loyal to Ron, but if any of them bothered to look deeper, they would see the bitter truth. I was damaged, flawed, and oh so very broken.

I was also trying to wrap my head around Declan replacing Alex. I knew it was going to happen, eventually. I knew Alex wasn't coming back, and that I was the reason he left, because I wasn't good enough, but somehow Dec working at the bar gave it a sense of finality, something I had been dreading. As long as he kept to himself, and stopped fucking staring, I would deal with it. Ron's word was law and there was nothing else I could do. The feeling of being powerless, yet again, is a vice on my chest, and I find myself taking a shuddering breath, feeling like I'm suffocating.

Things finally started winding down around one in the morning, and I actually had a moment of joy when I realized I wouldn't have to do the closing work all by myself for once. Ron always left from his private door around midnight, unless something big was happening, and the guys were always drunk or in the middle of luring a girl upstairs by the time closing came around. I rarely slept well, and was nearly at the point of exhaustion by this time of night. Ron had a cleaning service, but I still had to make sure everything was restocked, and that all the glasses were clean and ready for opening the next day.

Something There In Between

Quinn was completely wasted, sitting on the far end of the bar near Ron's office and he had been watching me all night, too. Unlike Declan, who seemed to be learning me, Quinn's gaze was predatory. Sitting on a stool, leaning on his right hand with his left arm resting on the bar, he was just staring. I knew he kind of had a small thing for me, but I also knew he wouldn't try anything because he was mostly a good guy, and there was an unspoken rule about leaving me alone. Besides, I had been here for four years, one of those years without Alex. I'm pretty sure if he was gonna try anything, he would have already. Tonight, though, there was an entirely different look in his eyes. It made a chill run up my spine. His eyes just didn't look right to me; something was off. I pushed those thoughts aside as I walked up to him, raising my eyebrows, silently asking if he wanted another. He was way past needing to be cut off in my opinion, but it was Ron's bar, and he was one of Ron's guys. He would get whatever he asked for.

"You's so pretty, Breeeeee," he slurs into his almost empty glass before downing the tiny bit left, and slamming the glass down so hard on the bar that I was amazed it didn't shatter.

"And you're drunk, Quinn," I mutter, beginning to wipe the bar top a little harder than necessary, avoiding eye contact, and becoming more and more uncomfortable by the second. *Please don't keep talking,* I mentally plead.

"I's so sorry he left, Breeeee. He's fuckin' sssstupid. You's knows if you was mine I wouldn't be lying to you like—" Quinn's drunken speech is abruptly interrupted when Ron walks up behind him, and grabs his shoulder, giving him a strong squeeze. I'm shocked Ron is still here this late. Quinn is so drunk it doesn't really faze him, but I can tell he gets the point because his eyes widen and his mouth snaps shut. Unfortunately, Ron wasn't quick enough to stop me from feeling the cold stab in my heart I feel every time Alex is brought up. Tears build up behind my eyes, and I take a deep breath trying to center myself. It wasn't enough that Alex had to show me how worthless I was to him; everyone here got a front seat view of just how little I was worth too. They all saw how easy it was to replace and forget me.

"Time to go to bed, Quinn. Why don't you go upstairs and sleep it off? Your drunk ass will never make it home on your own, and I got shit to do." Ron makes his point by squeezing Quinn's shoulder again.

"Sure thingssss," Quinn warbles while stumbling to his feet and walking with a distinct sway towards the kitchen door that leads to the bar's back exit, and ultimately the stairs behind the building to the second level.

I keep scrubbing the bar top with my rag, furiously, until Ron turns back to me and puts his hand on mine. I jump back and look up at him. He sighs, giving me the worst kind of look, the kind that is full of pity.

"Quinn's a drunk idiot. Don't pay attention to anything he says, kiddo," Ron says, looking at me with concern, as I use nothing but pure willpower to push the tears back. He looks like he wants to say something else, but I quickly cut him off.

"I know. No biggie." I shrug like it's nothing, and throw the rag into the pile on the floor to be washed. I turn to Declan, who is restocking the liquor shelf. He makes a show of looking busy, but I know he saw and heard everything. The way he's been silently observing me and the bar tonight, there is no way he just missed that.

"We're done for the night. Once you bag up the rags and towels, you can leave them in the alley for the cleaning company and head home. I'll see you tomorrow evening." I keep my eyes down, afraid of what he would see if I met his gaze, and then do a little half wave at him as I walk outside.

"Do you want me to walk you home?" Declan asks, looking far more concerned than I'm comfortable with.

He shoots a nervous glance towards Ron's office when he asks and it makes me wonder if he's been warned off of spending time with me.

"No, I'm good," I mutter, doing everything I can to dodge his insistent gaze.

I know I need to sleep, but on my cold walk home, Quinn's words are running through my head on a continuous loop.

"I'm sorry he left, Bree."

"He's an idiot, Bree."

"I'm so sorry, Bree."

The same phrases, over and over again, said to me by Quinn, Ron and a few of the other guys. Greg had even offered to break Alex's legs for me if I ever found him. I'm pretty sure Jake tried to break his legs once or twice before he even left. I think it had something to do with the circumstances when we started working for Ron, but none of that was Alex's fault. It was mine.

I don't know why everyone acts like Alex is the bad guy. He didn't do anything that anyone else wouldn't have done. He's not the villain of this story, I am. No one seems to realize that he left because of me. He left because I wasn't good enough. I wasn't the one that could do better; he was. He did. I know trying to sleep now would be a wasted effort, so I divert my path to the park.

Putting my earbuds in, I scroll through my phone until I find what I'm looking for, and as the melody hits me, I let the first tears fall.

Chapter 5

Declan

It didn't take a psychology degree to realize something Quinn said was a trigger for Bree. I had spent enough time seeing the same look on my mother's face to know. I was all too familiar with triggers myself: unlocked bedroom doors, people walking into my space without announcing themselves and sometimes even seeing a cop's nightstick was enough to make my mind fill with memories I never wanted to relive.

The face Bree made after Quinn's drunken speech was the face you make when you're trying to hide a terrible, terrible pain. I tried to run into Jake towards the end of the evening, but he was wasted out of his mind. I did manage to overhear a conversation between Jake and Ron while I pretended to give that side of the bar a deep cleaning.

"I know she only wanted that piece of shit back there with her, but she's getting overwhelmed and over worked. I've waited for him to get his shit together as long as I'm gonna. He's not welcome here anymore," Ron said, giving Jake a knowing look while Jake nodded his agreement.

"I don't know why you put up with his ass. Fucker was lazy and treated Bree like shit. Should have kicked his fucking ass before he left," Jake mumbled. I wanted him to elaborate, but just saying that had seemed like a monumental achievement in Jake's drunken state.

"Kiddo never had a shot with her fucked up life. I didn't get the chance to do right by my little girl but I'll be damned if Bree gets fucked over because her, well she's one of us." Ron actually seems disconcerted talking about his mysterious daughter.

I was fascinated that the rumors of Ron's long lost daughter seemed to be true, and I really wanted to know more about Alex, if only so I could use the information to hunt him down and beat the shit out of him after I told him what a monumental mistake he made in ditching Bree. His loss will be my gain.

I didn't know what happened after Ron took them in, but I guess they broke up, and the asshole left Bree behind. I don't need to know more than that. I can already tell she is better off. She is fucking gorgeous, and Ron cares about her, which means every motherfucker on his payroll cares about her. They weren't the greatest group of guys, but I'd rather have them with me than against me.

I nodded at Ron as I gave up my pretense of cleaning and headed to the backdoor, to drop the bags of dirty linens in the back alley. Would it kill them to have some fucking outdoor lighting? The crispness of fall brings heaviness in the air. It's my favorite time of year to be honest. If it weren't so late, I would have gone for a second run.

Something There In Between

I found my thoughts were staying on Bree as I walked, absent-mindedly kicking the occasional fallen leaf out of my way. She was definitely a loner, and I wasn't sure that was a good thing. Sometimes people stay alone because they think they don't deserve anything better. Those are the people that need help the most.

When Bree didn't think anyone was paying attention, she watched everyone laughing and hanging out with the same look on her face that a kid does looking through a toy store window. Why?

I made a mental note to try to talk to Ron about her, and then immediately changed my mind. He would probably break my kneecaps for just asking about her. It wasn't just that I was interested in her. I mean she's gorgeous and okay, I wanted her in the worst kind of way, but I'm mostly worried. She is someone in a world of pain, and she needs help before it consumes her...like it consumed my mom.

Thinking about Bree for ten minutes doesn't make it hard to decide where I want to go, so I'm standing across from the park again, Bree's park, just a few minutes later. I want to make sure she's ok. I *need* to know she's ok. I look towards the bench and see Bree sitting there. Something inside me says not to disturb her, so I stand like a creep under a street lamp watching her. She has her earbuds in; their white color is in stark contrast to her dark hair and black clothes, even in the dim light. She seems to be staring off into space, like she was when I saw her this afternoon. Her shoulders are shaking slightly, and I realize she's crying. Everything in me screams to comfort her... to shelter her and give her some of my strength. My inner caveman rears his head, wanting to throw her over my shoulder and take her home to keep the world from hurting her anymore.

I don't know how much time passes, but my legs are numb from the cold when she finally stands and starts to walk towards her building that I'm still standing in front of. Shit, she is going to think I'm such an asshole. She has her head down, and doesn't see me, until she's almost right on me.

She looks surprised to see me, but doesn't say anything, as she gives me a look so full of pain I have to clench my fists, digging my short nails into my palms, to keep from reaching for her. Her eyes are red and swollen; tear tracks from her mascara run down her cheeks. She looks so broken and beautiful. She holds my gaze for a moment, and beyond the pain I see something else, longing maybe? Does she want me to comfort her? I take a hesitant step towards her, but she gives a slight shake of her head and pushes past me, her shoulder briefly making contact with my bicep. I turn slightly, watching as she lets her head hang down again, and walks inside her building.

On my walk home, I mull over what just happened. We definitely just had some sort of moment, and my need to understand her, to help her, has increased by tenfold. She really was just sitting on a park bench at almost four in the morning, in the cold, crying her fucking eyes out. She is worse off than I thought. It would be easy to just assume this had to do with the ex, and I really do wonder what the fuck that bastard has done to her, but I have a feeling this goes much deeper.

S. Ferguson

Chapter 6

Bree

I wake up with another headache from crying so hard, even after I've come back inside from my bench. Usually I can hold my emotions in, and limit my crying to when I'm in the park, my safe place. On top of all that, knowing that Declan saw me crying last night makes my head hurt even more. I feel so incredibly vulnerable that he knows not only my special place, but how truly torn up I am inside. There was no way to hide my pain last night. Even the best warrior gets too tired to hold his shield up sometimes. Despite the fact that the park was technically public, I've never run into anyone there, much less anyone I know, before Declan. Was he following me? He had to have been, why else would he be there so late at night, and for the second time in such a short period of time? I feel a flash of anger that my private place has been found. I feel like I've been violated.

The park is my shelter, my safe place. If I can't go sit in the park, I don't know what else I can do to cope... if you want to call this coping.

After popping some Advil, and chugging a glass of orange juice, I distract myself with cleaning my already spotless apartment and doing laundry. The day passes quickly. To be fair, I woke up at noon, so there really wasn't too much of a day left anyway. As

I'm putting clean towels away in my linen closet, I find myself just staring at the closet. It's messy. I never saw the point in trying to fold fitted sheets, and I usually just reach in and grab what's on top when getting anything I need. I feel the surge of emotion in my chest right before I hear *her* voice echoing in my head.

"If you have your linen closet organized, that means you really have your life together," I hear her icy voice, dripping in judgment, in my head. "Does this look like you have your life together, Bree? Hmmm, does it?"

The last thing I need to think about right now is *her.*

"You're such a disaster, Bree. No one is ever going to want you. You're such a mess. Lazy, spoiled, selfish little bitch. You can't even keep one simple closet clean."

I close my eyes and sink to the floor of my bedroom, wrapping myself in a ball as I lay my cheek on the cold wooden floor as the memories flood my brain.

I haven't had a trigger hurt me as badly as Quinn's from last night did in a long time. My mind is moving at a furious pace, memory after memory flooding me. My view of reality is shifting, I can't tell what's real and what's not anymore. Everyone must know. All the guys... Ron. They must know what a fucking train wreck I am. Declan. I can't bear to think about what Declan must have realized about me last night.

I look over and see the one thing I took from Mother's house staring back at me. A single wadded up shirt, the last thing she ever bought me. It's something I never wear now and I don't know why I even brought the stupid frilly pink shirt. I don't even know why it's out of the closet. I walk up to it, picking it up carefully. As a reflex I begin to straighten it out, smoothing the wrinkles out. Suddenly, every painful memory I have is flooding my mind, and my chest feels like it's collapsing in on itself.

4 Years Ago

I rushed through the house frantically trying to make sure everything was in order. Mother would be home soon and there would be hell to pay if the house, and myself, didn't look perfect. She had a work dinner tonight, and was expecting me to go with her.

"Bree, where are you?" I hear her call as she walks through the front door, shutting it behind her.

I slowly walk into her view from the living room. I had been meticulous with my appearance, applying careful layers of foundation and concealer to hide the bruises on my cheek, making sure my dress had sleeves long enough to hide the bruises left from her grabbing my arms.

"You're not really expecting to go like that, are you?" she demands without having even looked at me. Her venom doesn't even sting right now. I learned a long time ago that I would never be good enough for her.

"I made sure my dress was ironed, and I spent 2 hours on my hair, Mother," I say in a quiet voice. I know any argument I make will be futile.

"Watch your attitude, you little bitch!" she hisses at me, taking a step forward, but stopping herself. She shoves a shopping bag at me and orders me to change into the frilly pink shirt and skinny jeans. I throw them on, hoping I look the way she wanted me to. We have to leave, and there is no time for me to fix my appearance if she takes her anger out on me now. I know this is only a temporary reprieve. She won't forget to punish me tonight when we come home.

"It's fine. Most of the staff know I have a fuck-up for a daughter already. Besides, we're out of time," she sighs, like she's making some sort of sacrifice by allowing me to accompany her.

Thankfully, she's silent most of the way to the restaurant. I am happy to be going to the dinner mainly because I know I'll eat tonight, and she's always somewhat nicer when there are people around. Yesterday had been my 16th birthday, which she had completely ignored, so I tell myself to just pretend tonight is my birthday dinner. I've learned to find joy in my imagination and comforting illusions.

Once we park, she plasters a fake smile on her face and grabs my hand, squeezing it to the point of pain, as we walk through the double doors of the restaurant. I can't fake smile as well as she can, but I make sure to keep my face in a pleasantly neutral expression despite wanting to grimace from the pain in my fingers. As soon as I smell all the food cooking, my stomach growls loudly. Mother shoots me a scathing look, and I promptly look at the floor. I want to tell her I wouldn't be so hungry if she left the fridge and pantry unlocked.

She always tells me I'm nothing but a horrible mistake from her past that won't go away. I'm the reason my father died. He left for a dangerous job because I was another mouth to feed. I'm the reason he put himself at risk and lost his life. Such a heavy burden to thrown on a child, but her insults and blame don't end there. She never hesitates to tell me that I am fat and need to watch how much I eat, that we don't have money for me to be eating all the time like the lazy and greedy person I am. The reality is, I only get breakfast and lunch on school days, and even those are light meals because they're only possible due to generous people who see me without anything and offer to share their food. Miss Karen, one of the lunch ladies, always sneaks me as much of a meal as she can after the lunch-line dies down. Some days, there isn't enough food, though. My ribs protrude from my chest, and I know I'm far past underweight. It does work to my advantage because my clothes are all about a size too small. I know that if I were at a healthy weight, most of them would be un-wearable. It's also delayed my menstrual cycle starting, which, from what I hear, is a blessing.

We approach the table of her coworkers, and they stand to greet us. I give a tightlipped smile back to most of the greetings. I know I'm not allowed to really speak to these people, and take a seat next to my mother. They begin talking about ordering appetizers, and someone asks me if I want something specific.

"She doesn't need an appetizer. Silly thing forgot we had the dinner tonight so she'd already eaten when I got home from work. She'll just have a salad," my mother interjects, adding on a fake laugh. I see some of her coworkers raise their eyebrows at Mother's statement, but she continues as if she hasn't noticed. Soon, their talk drifts back to work related topics.

Twenty minutes later, everyone is enjoying shrimp and bread and a mixture of other food as I slowly munch on my salad. I feel pressure on my hand, and realize someone is pushing something into my right hand. Startled, I look up and meet the eyes of one of mother's friendlier coworkers; I think her name is Karen. She gives me an intense look, and pushes down on my hand again. I turn my palm up, and realize she's pressing a roll into my hand. I panic internally, and try to come up with a quick plan. I look at Mother, waiting for her to stop speaking for a moment. When she does, I politely ask to be excused to the restroom.

"Sure, I'll take you," my mom says, starting to rise from her chair. I freeze, and panic shoots through my veins.

"Wait, Elizabeth, you were going to tell me how that meeting with Bill went," Karen says, and I could kiss her.

"Well," my mom hesitates. I know I'll most likely pay for this later, but the momentary reprieve is worth it.

"Bree is more than old enough to go to the bathroom by herself," Karen says, dismissing me, before launching questions at Mother about the meeting.

I quickly run to the bathroom, and stuff the whole roll into my mouth before washing my hands and making sure to count until I know 5 minutes have passed. If I go back to the table too quickly, or if I take too long, Mother will be more suspicious.

As I'm exiting the bathroom, I crash into what feels like a brick wall. I nearly fall backwards from the impact, but two strong hands shoot out and grip my biceps, keeping me steady.

"What's the rush?" a deep voice asks, and I look up into the two most beautiful, deepest blue eyes I have ever seen. They look like the ocean when you're far out at sea.

"I'm so sorry," I murmur, still mesmerized by his eyes.

He gives me a cocky grin, those beautiful eyes swirling with amusement, and releases my arms. He takes a step back from me, and gives me an appraising look up and down. His hair is long and wild on the top of his head, and shaved on the sides. He doesn't look like anyone I've ever met before. He looks dangerous.

"Just be careful. You're too small to be running into people," he says, as he pats me on the head like you would a small child before turning around and walking into the men's room.

I shake my head to clear the daze the whole encounter caused, and make my way back to the table.

My mother shoots me a suspicious glance, but I pretend not to see it, as I resume eating my salad. At least, she let me have salad dressing this time.

"Bree, I'm so glad you're back. My son showed up after all, and I can't wait to introduce you two," Karen says, when I sit back down at the table.

I smile and nod in polite agreement, as Mother reaches under the table on the left side and pinches my thigh.

I grimace and lean towards her. "Don't think I don't know what you're up to!" she hisses in my ear.

Honestly, I have no idea what she thinks I'm up to. I doubt she noticed me sneak the roll, so she's probably made something up in her head to have yet another reason to justify the way she'll punish me tonight. With a hopeless and exhausted sigh, I resume eating my salad. Sometimes, I feel like I should just stop pretending everything is okay.

Even after years of trying to please her, making sure I never embarrass her in public, she still beats me every time we come home. I'm never going to be good enough. I just can't do it.

I'm startled out of my thoughts when there is movement to my right. I notice Karen has moved her seat down and none other than the mysterious boy from the bathroom is now taking the seat to my right.

"Bree this is my son, Alex," Karen says, a huge grin on her face.

Alex looks at me with a smile. "We already ran into each other."

Present Day

As quickly as it hit me, the flashback ends and I'm hurtled back into the midst of my panic attack. Tears fall, and I curl my body into a tighter ball, struggling to get air into my lungs. *Please stop. Please stop. Go away.* I repeat over and over again in my head, eventually saying the words out loud.

Oh, God, please help me.

I don't know how much time passes before I finally manage to slow my breathing, and calm some of the madness in my head. I am still curled up on the floor of my bedroom, face pressed against the cold wood floor. It's getting harder and harder to get a grip and to focus, when the memories flood my brain. I'm pretty sure that was a panic attack, but I'm not prepared to do anything about them. Panic attacks mean you need medication and counselors. I've read about them briefly before, when I first had an incident after Alex left. I've always been too scared to talk to anyone, especially a professional, about my past. The one thing I do know is that I am slowly being consumed. Inside of me, there is a small part that says I need to give up. I cannot continue to live this way, trying to keep a grip on reality, to hold myself together. It's too much.

When I think about everyone else around me, it seems like I'm the only one still paying the price. Alex has clearly moved on and is living a happier life. Mother never reported me as a runaway, or even looked for me, so obviously her life is now better without me in it. Ron and his guys all keep their distance from me, like I'm some sort of crazy person. Even though I know I am the one who has pushed everyone away, there is a part of me that wishes someone would fight for me, even if I'm the one they have to fight.

I shake my head, clearing my depressing thoughts away. It works, but I know it's only temporary as I rise to my feet. The need to do something, to distract myself, is strong. I pull my phone out to go through my messages and, for the first time, I pause. Do I really want to go have another meaningless encounter? I know, as much as they provide temporary relief, they're only making a deep hole deeper. My heart doesn't exist anymore, just a large black hole. I've never really stopped to think about it before. I know that I'm being used, but I rationalize this with the fact that I'm using them as well. I hurry up and send a few messages out before I can second-guess myself again. As usual, Nate is the first to respond. I take a quick shower, dressing for the shift at the bar I have later, and head to his house.

He opens the door wearing nothing but a pair of gym shorts when I arrive. "Twice in a week. I knew you couldn't resist this dick," he says, while crudely grabbing his crotch.

I roll my eyes and push past him to walk to his room. Once there, I start systematically stripping. I have to keep my clothes neat since I can't just go home after this.

"What's the rush, baby?" Nate asks as he walks in the room and shuts his door behind him. I notice he flicks the lock. That's not something he usually does, but it doesn't seem like a big deal, so I don't say anything.

"I didn't come here to talk," I reply, pulling off my underwear. Completely naked now, I crawl up on his bed and lay down on my side, facing him.

He gives my body a slow once over. He's already hard, his gym shorts hide nothing, and so I put on my best seductive face, motioning him forward with my fingers. If I didn't know better, I would think he actually does think I'm desirable.

He yanks his gym shorts down his legs, his cock springing free and slapping up against his lower stomach. He tries to immediately lie between my legs, but I make a sound of protest, and raise one eyebrow when his eyes meet mine.

"Oh, come on, why do I always have to wear a condom? I'm clean, baby." His voice is all nasally and whiny in tone.

"Am I the only person you're sleeping with?" I already know the answer.

He remains silent, and averts his gaze.

"That's what I thought. Put on the damn condom," I demand.

Once he's sheathed himself, he enters me in one rough thrust, and I grunt from the impact and the brief pain. He starts up a steady rhythm, and I let my mind go. The only sound in the room is his grunting and the sound of our skin makes while smacking together. I stare at the ceiling for a few moments. My heart aches. *Alex, my Alex, why did you leave me?* Usually, if I think of him during this, I can stop myself. I must still be weak from my panic attack earlier. The one thing that I had only ever shared with him I now share with many. But I can't stop. I can't *not* sleep with Nate. I can't stand the idea of no human contact. I'm not good for much else, but I can do this. Guys don't mind sleeping with me. It's the only affection I'll ever get, so I have to take it. There's still a part of me that feels like this is cheating. I feel another piece break off inside of me, another chunk of my soul dying.

I don't know what else I can do. I don't know how to be anything else, but this monster. I used to imagine having to beg Alex's forgiveness if he came back and found out what I have done. But, now I know I won't even be able to forgive myself. Sometimes, the damage inside us becomes so great that it consumes us, and the only way we can begin to cope is by continuing to add to the damage until it's all we have inside of us.

The solitude of my thoughts is shattered when Nate wraps a hand around my neck and squeezes. Hard. I open my eyes and gasp. His eyes are cold, staring straight into mine, unwavering. I've never seen Nate look like this before, but I am far too familiar with the look in someone's eyes when they intend to hurt you. I've seen the focused rage in his eyes many, many times before. Adrenaline rushes through my veins, and I try to find a way to fight back.

I try to scream, but the sound is weak and muffled from the lack of oxygen. My lungs are burning, desperate for oxygen. I try my best to sit up, but the move is futile. Nate outweighs me by at least fifty pounds. I shove at Nate's chest, trying to get him off of me, another useless effort. He slides down my body a little, but his hand on my throat only squeezes harder. With the little bit of space his movement gives me, I bring my knee up to connect with his body. There isn't much strength behind the movement, but I feel my knee connect hard with his groin.

"What the fuck?" Nate roars, rolling off me to the side, which is actually the edge of the bed and, as he falls off, his arms flail and his hand connects with my cheek. It's an almost perfect backhanded slap. Believe me, I know backhanded slaps.

I don't even pause, jumping off the bed, and putting as much distance between Nate and me as I can, rubbing my throat, trying to soothe the ache from his grip.

"What the fuck was that shit?" Nate looks at me, his eyes almost look manic. For a moment, I wonder if he's taken something, or has he just gone crazy?

He was the one choking me. He was the one that wouldn't stop. I couldn't breathe; he was killing me.

I keep backing up, trying to put as much space between us as I can. It feels like my cheek is on fire. There is no way a hit that hard isn't going to leave a mark.

Judging from the ache in my neck, I probably have marks there, too. This is just fantastic. Ron will not be amused when I show up for work looking like shit. No one will be. The idea of explaining myself or my *activities* to anyone scares the shit out of me. Declan's face pops into my head, but I ignore that thought just as quickly as it appears.

Something There In Between

"You have some goddamn nerve yelling at me. Why were you choking me? I couldn't breathe asshole. That's what happened," I shout back, keeping my eyes on him and walking sideways toward my neatly folded pile of clothes sitting on his dresser.

"Oh, no, you fucking don't," Nate shouts as he lunges through the short distance between us, and grips my arm.

"What the fuck are you doing?" I scream, trying to swing my free arm to strike him, but he quickly moves behind me, twisting the arm he's holding behind my back and uses his other hand to grip my hair. It feels like all the hair is being ripped out of my head and my shoulder is dangerously close to getting dislocated as he shoves me face first into the bed. My legs are still on the ground, and I blindly kick backwards. I connect with his shin, and hear a grunt, before his grip on my hair gets impossibly tighter. He jerks my head the side, and lowers his mouth to my ear.

"Do that shit again, and I'll really fuck you up. I'm not done yet, so you fucking sit there like a good little bitch and take it. I'll let you go when I'm good and fucking ready." His voice is a whisper, a calm, infuriating whisper. He bites my ear lobe. Hard. Tears fall from my eyes, as I scream and thrash against him. I try to clamp my legs together as tight as I can, but he wedges his thigh between them forcing my legs open. He's so much stronger than me. The feeling of being so helpless does nothing but increase my rage. Angry tears roll down my face.

Please God, please. For once, can you just save me? I don't know why I expect a response this time; he's never shown up before.

Nate shoves himself harshly into my body; it feels like I'm being ripped in half. I stop moving and close my eyes, continuing to sob in my defeat. My only hope is that this will be over soon. My face slides against the bed with every thrust, the smell of his dirty sheets floods my senses with every breath I take. I'll never be able to smell his cologne again without remembering this moment. I can tell he's getting close to finishing because his thrusts become more frantic, and he pushes down harder on the back of my head. If he pushes my head any harder into the mattress, I won't be able to breathe.

When he finishes, he slaps my ass and he releases his hold on me. I'm still crying, quiet sobs shaking my entire body. My head hurts, my entire body hurts. The worst pain is the burn in my chest. My mind is reeling, trying to grasp what just happened. I know I'm at risk of going into shock, but I have to get out of here.

Nate never says a word, as I stumble across his room to grab my clothes before making my way into his bathroom. The harsh florescent lighting hurts my eyes when I flick the switch. I look at my face in the mirror, and don't recognize the hollow face looking back at me. My eyes are red and swollen as I continue to cry. My lip is split, and a small trickle of blood runs down my chin. I don't even remember that happening. I must have bitten it during… during what happened.

The bruise on my cheek is getting darker by the second. My neck is red, but it doesn't look like it's going to bruise. My arm is a completely different story. I can see the perfect imprint of Nate's hand turning into a bruise. My earlobe has the perfect imprint of his teeth on it, already starting to darken to a bruise as well. That won't be fading away anytime soon. I adjust my body to lean closer to the mirror, and get a better look at my face when I feel it. Pure horror rushes through me when I feel the stickiness between my thighs. Nate took the condom off.

Just another thing he took away from me tonight. My stomach rolls with disgust at Nate. At myself. I don't even know who to blame for this. I collapse on the cold linoleum floor, even more tears falling. You would think I would eventually just run out of tears. I'm not sure how much time passes before Nate bangs on the door roughly, startling me.

"You need to leave. My girlfriend called and wants to stop by," he says, gruffly, before walking away from the door. I stand weakly, keeping my mouth shut. I simply don't have the strength to deal with this further insult added to injury.

I hear the sounds of him moving around his room, probably straightening up. I clean myself up as best as I can, cringing when I see the red and pink stains on the toilet paper. I'm bleeding, but I don't have time to think about this right now, I need to leave. I'm not in pain yet, but I know it's coming. If I can make it to work before it gets too bad, I know Ron always keeps painkillers on hand. A lot of the guys get injuries that they can't be seen at the hospital for. I dress, being gentle, and moving so very slowly. I walk out and Nate's room looks like none of this just happened. He's changed his sheets and lit a candle; the smell of flowers is overwhelming. Nate isn't in his room, and I know I don't want to see him again, now or ever.

I quickly exit his house, and make my way down the sidewalk, heading to Keegan's. I'm limping slightly, the pain between my legs increasing with each step. As I walk, I try to decide how I'm going to explain this. I wish for once I had a car because a car accident seems like the only way I can explain so many injuries. If I tell Ron what happened, he's going to be angry. I don't know if he would go after Nate, but he'll be angry at me for putting myself in a situation that could involve cops. The reality of the situation continues to crash down on me. I just let a guy rape me. Was that rape? Is it rape if you were there to sleep with the guy anyway? I feel so confused. It feels so wrong, but something inside me is saying, *What did you think would happen? You're only good for one thing.*

I was there willingly. I just changed my mind because he started hurting me. What do I do? What am I supposed to do? No one would believe me anyway. I've been sleeping with Nate off and on for a few months now.

That's because you are a whore, a worthless whore… a voice reminds me. As much as I hide the reality of who I am from everyone else, I'll never be able to hide it from myself.

I arrive at Keegan's much earlier than I anticipated, especially with my limp, so I decide to have a smoke by the door, and keep trying to come up with a cover story. My mind seems stuck on the pain. I've just put my lighter back in my pocket when Declan rounds the corner. He greets me with a smile. Then, I see the exact moment he realizes something is wrong. My last thought before he reaches me is that his face is beautiful, even when it contorts with rage.

"WHAT THE FUCK?" he roars, reaching between us and cradling my chin. Despite his anger, his touch is gentle. I almost want to lean into his hand for comfort. His reaction means my face must look worse now than it did when I left Nate's house. Despite it being four years since I last had someone beat me, I have spent far longer dealing with bruises and injuries on a daily basis than not. I still know how to tune the pain out, and some habits don't go away easily, especially habits that help you survive.

"It was an accident," I try to placate him. Declan looks furious, his green eyes are blazing, his nostrils flaring and his chest is heaving. Furious Dec is a fearsome and beautiful sight to behold.

"Sure 'it was an accident,'" he says, making air quotations.

"Look, it was an accident. I don't want to talk about it." I keep my tone matter of fact, only realizing after the last word leaves my mouth that's only going to make it worse.

"A fucking accident?" Declan asks me, his face a mask of disbelief.

"Yes, let's just leave it at that." I drop my cigarette to the ground and stomp it out. I wince from the movement before I can catch myself.

"You're fucking hurt!" Declan says, his voice has more concern than anger now. I can tell he isn't going to drop this. Why oh why did he have to be the first person I ran into tonight?

Declan holds the door to Keegan's open for me, and I limp in front of him. I hear his sharp intake of breath when he notices. He's going to make a big deal out of this. For the second time tonight, I feel utterly powerless.

Ron is just walking out of his office...talk about the worst fucking timing. He raises an eyebrow at seeing Declan and I walk in together, but doesn't say anything. Yet again, I see the exact moment when Ron spots my face and awkward gait. His head snaps back in my direction, and I swear I hear him growl, as he storms over to me. If furious Declan is a thing of beauty, furious Ron is terrifying. He almost looks like an avenging angel storming toward me with the lights and smoke in the bar creating a hazy glow around him. I wonder how many people have seen this same image: Ron storming toward them, his face full of anger, and it was the last thing they ever saw?

"The fuck?" he says, his voice is cold as ice. I've seen Ron angry quite a few times, but I've definitely never seen him go arctic before.

"That's what I said," Declan says, walking to stand next to Ron, so they're both facing me with their arms crossed over their chests. I know they're ganging up on me, but I'm so weak. I can't match them, not now. I hunch my shoulders in defeat and decide to make one last, albeit futile, attempt at avoiding this conversation.

"Look, it was an accident, I'm fine. I just need some meds, and I'll be good as new." I give them a strained smile. I remember my split lip too late, and feel it tear open followed by a trickle of blood flowing down my chin from the re-opened wound.

The fury in Ron's eyes doesn't diminish in the slightest at my pathetic explanation.

"You," he points at me. "In my office now. You're gonna tell me who the fuck is responsible for this. Then, Jake and Greg are going to make sure his face matches yours before they cut his dick off." With that, Ron walks off in the direction of his office and I limp my way behind him. Holy shit! This is not how I wanted tonight to go.

Ron points at one of the leather overstuffed chairs across from his desk once we're inside and he shuts the door. I gingerly lower myself down, trying not to whimper as my lower half finally connects with the soft leather. He surprises me by taking the chair next to me, instead of his usual spot behind his desk. He takes a few deep breaths before he looks at me again.

"You can lie to anyone else you want to, but do not fucking lie to me. I know a woman who's been raped when I see one. I won't pretend I know what this is like for you. I'm not gonna make you go to the cops, and drag this out if you don't want to, but you need to tell me who did this." I open my mouth to protest, but Ron keeps talking. "You don't have to tell me anything other than his name, but you will tell me." He gives a deep sigh, seeming to rethink some of what he just said. "If you really want to go to the cops, we can do that, too. I'll stay with you the whole way. It's your choice, but one of those two is happening. Tonight." He gives me a look that makes my heart ache. For a moment, I feel safe. I feel cared for.

Then, I remember this is just business. Ron can't let someone get away with hurting one of his employees. It would make him look weak.

"What are you going to do if I give you his name?" I'm pretty sure I know the answer, but I want to hear him say it.

"Kill him." Ron doesn't hesitate. He looks me right in the eyes as he speaks.

"I...I don't even think it was really rape. I mean I've been...I've been *seeing* him for a while now and things were just...they were just different this time." I stumble through the words, trying to not tell Ron more than I need to. Every word makes scenes from earlier run through my mind. My hand drifts up to gently rub my neck as I remember Nate's hard grip. I can almost hear his heavy breathing and grunting. I shudder involuntarily, my stomach rebels, and for a moment, I think I might be sick.

"If you have to even think about whether it was rape or not, it fucking was. I don't care if you're married to the motherfucker, living in a house with a white picket fence and shit. If he hurt you, if he touched you without your permission, if he keeps going when you say stop, it's fucking rape." Ron's tone is absolute. "Give me his name. I promise it won't come back on you, and I promise he'll never touch you again."

"You're asking me to kill someone." Ron opens his mouth, but I raise my hand to stop him. "I can't give you his name knowing you're going to kill him. Even if it is rape, like you said, I can't just let you kill him." My eyes are watering, and I know I'm about to start crying, again. It feels like that's all I do anymore. I haven't cried in front of Ron since the first night he met me. I was crying tears of joy that night, to finally have food in my stomach, and a place to sleep; it almost feels like I've come full circle in a twisted way.

"If you don't want me to kill him, I can't agree to that. I can promise that it won't come back on you, and I promise that I would kill anyone who attacked one of mine; it's not just you. But, kiddo, you deserve revenge for this. I would bring you his head if I didn't think it would do you more harm than good to see. He's going to pay. You're one of us, and no one fucks with us." Ron leans back in his chair, waiting for my answer.

I know this is the best I'll get from Ron. Honestly, would the death of Nate really matter on my conscious? I'm already so fucked up. It's too late for me.

"I will give you his name." I give in.

I know no one is letting this go, and I don't want to go through the humiliation of being interviewed and examined by the police. I doubt they would have Ron's view of the situation anyway. I can almost hear their laughter when I tell the police someone I've been sleeping with willingly for months raped me. I know from too many painful experiences that the people who are supposed to be our heroes are really the villains. There are no more heroes in this world, at least not in mine.

"Good. Now, who is this bastard?" Ron leans forward, putting his forearms on his knees.

"Nate, Nate Richardson." I hate to admit it, but I feel a sense of relief telling Ron his name.

Ron gives me a curt nod, pulls his phone out of his pocket, and brings it to his ear.

"Jake. You with Greg? " He goes silent for a minute. I can hear Jake talking on the other line, but I can't make out what he's saying. "Good," Ron pauses, and puts his mouth over his phone before speaking to me.

"Go into my private bathroom. There's a change of clothes in the closet. They will be big on you, but it's better than nothing. Take a shower. Meds are in the cabinet, and take the bottle with you when you leave. I'm sending you home with Declan. You need to rest, and you can't be alone right now, until we find this fucker." I open my mouth to protest, but he gives me a hard look, and I close my mouth.

A few moments later, I'm standing under the hot water in Ron's shower. The water soothes my aches and the tension in my body. I carefully wash between my legs, wincing as the soap and water burn slightly. I get a weak sense of satisfaction when I'm finished, knowing I've washed all of Nate off of me.

True to what he said, Ron has a closet in his bathroom full of sweats and t-shirts. I grab the smallest I can find of each and dress. I use a comb to detangle my hair and throw on the hoodie I found hanging on the back of the door. When I walk back into his office, Declan is waiting for me. He's standing next to the leather chairs, his arms are crossed over his chest, and his legs are spread apart. He looks so big and intimidating. I never realized how tall he was before. He has to have at least a foot on my 5'4". His muscles are bulging under his black t-shirt, his tattoos peeking out from under the sleeves where they begin and continuing down his arms to his wrists. His long dark hair is loose, flowing around his head. If I let myself focus, I could picture him as a medieval knight.

"Did Ron tell you?" My voice is quiet. I play with the hem of the hoodie I'm wearing, looking anywhere but at Declan's face.

"He told me enough. He's on his way to meet up with Jake and Greg." I'm shocked Ron is leaving to handle this himself. He rarely handles anything personally anymore. I'm distracted from my thoughts by the way Declan's tone sounds almost envious. Why would he wish he were going? He's probably just upset that he's stuck here babysitting me.

"What about the bar?" If Declan's leaving with me, that means there's no bartender.

"Quinn's got it." Declan eyes are searching my face.

Something There In Between

"Look, you don't have to stay with me. I just need to go home and sleep. Ron's got the good stuff." I give a weak laugh, and jiggle the bottle of pain pills I took from Ron's cabinet that's now in the pocket of the hoodie.

"Yeah," Declan gives a sigh. "You do need sleep, but you're not going home. Ron said to take you to my place in case that fucker shows at your house. It won't take too long for word to get out that Ron's looking for him, but it's still going to take some time for them to track him down. If he gets wind they're looking for him, the asshole would probably head straight for your place. The last thing you need right now is to be alone. So, we can do this the easy way or we can do this the hard way, but you're going to my place. You're gonna rest, and I'm gonna keep an eye on you." Declan gives me what I think is supposed to be a stern look, but all I can think about is how beautiful he is. Again. What the fuck is wrong with me? What kind of fucked up person thinks someone is beautiful so soon after what happened? I must really be some sort of whore.

"Now that you're out, I'm gonna call a cab. You hungry? I can call and have something delivered if you want?" Declan has his phone out now, and is scrolling through it.

"I'm not hungry. I could use a drink, though." I toss my clothes in Ron's trashcan. I feel bad because it's a small trashcan, meant for paperwork, but I just can't stand the idea of bringing them home or wearing them again. Part of me wishes I could burn them.

"I have vodka. That work for you?" Declan asks before speaking to the cab company.
I nod shifting from foot to foot, trying to ignore how uncomfortable standing is, while he gives the address to the dispatcher, and ends the call before sliding his phone back into his pocket.

"Alright. There's a guy right around the corner, so it's our lucky night. Let's roll." Declan walks toward me. Carefully, he reaches over and pulls the hood over my head and zips the hoodie up as far as it goes. His eyes look so full of... something that I'm scared to name, and the gesture is so tender. "You don't wanna be outside in this cold with wet hair. You'll get sick." He grabs my purse from where I left it on the floor, and makes his way to Ron's private door.

"We can't use that. It's for Ron's use only," I recite the rule I was taught when Ron hired me. I don't know why something so trivial bothers me, but it does. There are rules in place that we have to follow. I can't take any more chaos or disorder tonight.

"I have permission from the big guy, special circumstances and all," Declan says before pushing the door open.

He was right about the cold air, it hits me and I start shivering uncontrollably. Declan walks straight to the cab, sitting in the alley, and opens the door for me. I slide in, wincing again as my ass hits the bench seat. Declan slides in next to me, sitting a little closer than normal, but not touching me. I get a whiff of his cologne, and it's a welcome relief from the smell of stale cigarettes that seems to be so permanent in all cabs.

The ride to Declan's apartment is so short I would have said taking a taxi was ridiculous if I weren't in so much pain. The relief from my shower is fading away, and exhaustion is kicking in.

I check out my surroundings while Declan pays the driver. His building looks like a typical apartment building, rows of windows with different types of blinds, and a few window boxes with dead plants in them. I also recognize the area; he's very close to me and my park. Maybe he wasn't following me that night. He types in a code, and the door to the building buzzes open. He opens it, and stands to the side, letting me go in first.

"My apartment is on the second floor. Can you make it up the stairs? If not, I can carry you?" He looks deep into my eyes when he asks this. I think he wants to make sure I'm not lying.

"I'm okay if I take it slowly." I make my way up the stairs, one step at a time, breathing deeply every time I have to raise a leg. Maybe I should have seen a doctor? I decide I don't care; it's nothing fatal, and the pain isn't worth the further humiliation.

Declan follows behind me patiently. I know he could probably have made it up in half the time, but he doesn't look irritated. "It's this one." Declan points toward the first door on the right, number thirty-two. I give a snort when I see the number.

"What's up with the snort? My door ugly or something?" Declan asks while using his key to unlock the door.

"Would you believe that thirty-two is my lucky number?"

"Yeah, I would believe that B Girl," Declan says, mysteriously, as I follow him into the apartment. It's pretty small, almost the same size as my studio, but he has a bedroom with an actual door. The floors are old, damaged wood, but he has a large rug in the living room area that gives it a cozy feeling. He doesn't have a couch, but an oversized leather loveseat instead. All the colors are neutral, and his walls are bare except for a huge flat screen TV mounted to the wall in front of the loveseat.

"Alright, B Girl, did you take any pills yet?" Declan asks, walking into his kitchen and rummaging around in some cabinets. I see him open his freezer and pull out a bottle of vodka.

"Not yet, I was waiting until I could sleep. Those things always knock me out." I slowly lower myself onto the loveseat.

"That works out perfectly because the plan is for you to pass out, so take them with this and get comfy." Declan hands me a double shot of vodka. "That's all you're getting. You know, mixing pain pills with alcohol and all that jazz..." I should probably find his sarcasm and upbeat attitude irritating, but it's so refreshing. He doesn't treat me like I'm broken, or like I'm damaged, even tonight of all nights.

I down the drink and a few pills in two swallows. Feeling the burn in my throat is a welcome distraction from all the other aches and pains in my body right now.

"You want the bed, or do you want to sleep on this thing?" he asks, sitting down next to me.

"I don't want to sleep yet. Can we watch TV?" I kick my shoes off, and curl my legs up beside me, wedging them in between Declan and me.

"We can do whatever you want. Here's the remote. I'm gonna change into something comfortable." Declan stands and walks to the door I'm assuming leads to the bedroom.

He shuts it behind him, and I use the remote to turn the TV on. I'm still randomly flipping through channels when he comes back out. He's changed into grey sweatpants, which hang low on his hips, and a tight white t-shirt. Holy hell, he's ripped. I can see the definition of his pecs and abs through the thin material. The dark ink of his tattoos is showing through as well. He definitely has a lot more on his chest and shoulders than I thought.

"Find anything good?" he asks, taking his seat next to me again.

"Nah, my eyes are getting tired. You find something." I toss him the remote, and lean my head back on the soft headrest. My eyes droop lower and lower and, before I know it, I'm sound asleep.

Chapter 7

Declan

Bree fell asleep pretty quickly after I sat back down next her. I debated leaving her where she was but figured she would be more comfortable on the bed. It meant a shitty night of no sleep for me. I was way too big to try to sleep on the loveseat, but she was worth it. Anger shoots through my body as I remember what Ron told me.

"Some fucker put his hands on her. More than his hands if you know what I'm saying." Ron had looked so angry and so sad in that moment. Whatever Bree thought of their relationship, Ron cared about her. There was no doubt in my mind after tonight. As much as I hated Jake's job sometimes, for once I was grateful he was a dangerous man. I was grateful Ron was a man not to be fucked with. He would make sure Bree got justice.

I had no doubt that Jake and Greg would make sure that motherfucker never hurt anyone again. He wouldn't know what hit him when Jake finds him. After everything our father did to Jake, the chance to avenge a victim of sexual assault is like a present. At first, I was disappointed to not be able to have a chance to help kill the fucker, but taking care of Bree was priority. Maybe she would let me in a little after I showed her what it was like to be cared for…that not everyone viewed her as a broken person or just a piece of ass.

Bree starts to snore lightly, and I snicker. Under better circumstances, she would be getting teased mercilessly about that when she woke up. Once she starts drooling on the cushion, I decide it's time to move her. The caveman inside of me is happy she's going to be in my bed, happy that she is wrapped in my scent, marking her as mine, safe and protected. I carefully pick her up. She's so light, too light, and make my way to the bedroom. Thankfully, today was laundry day, so I had changed my sheets earlier. I lay her in the middle of the bed, and pull the blanket over her. I don't know what it's like to go through what she did tonight, but I remember a few things I've noticed about Jake over the years. I leave the bathroom light on, so the room isn't completely dark, and leave the bedroom door cracked as well. I don't want her waking up in the dark, confused and feeling like she's trapped. Once I'm back on the loveseat, I decide to text Jake and see if he has any news.

You find the fucker?

I flip the channel to sports highlights while I'm waiting. I don't even like sports, but the background noise is a welcome distraction. My phone buzzes, and I throw the remote down and grab it.

Almost at his house now. You know he has a girlfriend? Her brother was the one who told us where to find him.

So, Bree was the side chick? From what I know about her, that isn't shocking. She clearly has no idea of her worth. I completely believe she would settle for being some dude's fallback. She doesn't seem to know she deserves so much more. She deserves to be someone's number one. She deserves to have a guy worship the ground she walks on. I know tonight is going to set her back. Ron told me she said she wasn't even sure if it was rape or not. I know, in my gut, Bree's going to put this on herself; she's going to refuse to blame anyone else. I'm not a perfect man, but I know what it's like to go through hell, and live to talk about it. I can be the man that she needs. I can show her exactly how worthy she is. I can be the person to save her from herself.

With my mind made up, I close my eyes and start to form a plan. Bree isn't going to make this easy.

A scream cuts through the quiet of my apartment, startling me from my uncomfortable sleep in the living room. It takes me a second to get my bearings and, before I can move, another scream, this one louder, comes from my bedroom. Bree. I jump over the back of the loveseat, reducing the trip to my bedroom door to only two large steps. Bree is curled into a small ball, her back against the wall next to the bed, screaming. Her eyes are closed, and I'm not sure if she's awake or not.

"Bree." I say her name in a low and calm tone. I don't want her to panic even more when she hears my voice. I've had my fair share of injuries from trying to wake Jake up from his nightmares. I doubt Bree can hit as hard as him, but I don't want to find out.

She whimpers, and tries to push herself further against the wall. I have no idea what to do. Jake had nightmares and flashbacks a lot, but he knows me; my voice is a comfort to him. Bree doesn't have that luxury.

Fuck it. I make my way across the room, and put a hand on her ankle.

"Bree, you're having a bad dream. Can you wake up?" I give her ankle a little shake, and her eyes shoot open. Blue eyes full of agony and unshed tears. "Hey, you had a nightmare. It's okay, though. I've got you," I say softly. I give her ankle another reassuring squeeze and, before I can move my hand, she launches her tiny body at me.

Her arms go around my neck, her face burrowing into my shoulder. I wrap both my arms around her without a single thought. I doubt she's fully awake, or aware of what she's doing, but even in her sleep her body knows she needs comfort. I'm not sure how long I sit there holding her, but her soft snores reach my ears again right about when my ass starts going numb from the hard floor. I'm scared to move, the last thing I want is to disturb her again. For all my discomfort and the fucked up events of the night, I can't help but think how right this feels to me. Bree in my arms. Safe. Protected. I can be that guy. I will be that guy.

When the numbing in my ass gets to the point I can't ignore it anymore, I use all the strength in my legs to raise myself up to one knee, then use my other leg to stand up. For once, I'm grateful she's underweight as I stumble to the bed and start to lay her down. She moves slightly and mumbles something I can't understand. Her arms are still around my neck, pulling me down as I lower her.

With a start her eyes open, blue eyes staring into mine, unseeing for a few seconds, before I see them focus. She flinches and throws herself backwards away from me, causing her to hit the mattress and bounce up. She scoots away from me until her back hits the wall. I give a deep sigh, and run my hands through my hair. As if the poor girl didn't have enough going on in her life, this shit had to happen to her. I hope Jake doesn't just kill that fucker. I hope he suffers. I debate sending him a text, telling him precisely that, but I don't want to leave to find my phone. I gently sit on the bed, my back resting against my pillow, and cross my arms over my chest. Still not comfortable, but better than the floor or the living room. The last thing I see before I doze off is Bree closing her eyes and going back to sleep herself.

The next morning, we're sitting on the loveseat again, both of us staring into our coffee cups when I decide that if I want to have Bree open up to me, I need to open up to her a little bit.

Despite our awkward silence this morning, I can sense she's now relaxed around me some. The tension in her shoulders isn't from me. When it comes to the past, Jake and I are complete opposites in the way we handle it, despite sharing so much of it. I don't mind talking about it, except for the last night with our father. There are reasons that night can never be spoken of, and most of them aren't mine. Most of our past, especially my memories of my mom, I feel like I need to talk about. I refuse to be silent and feel ashamed for the actions of my dad. I want my mom's memory to carry on, no matter how tainted it might be.

"You're looking a little better than last night," I say, stumbling my way through finding a way to bring up the heavy stuff without Bree knowing what's coming. I know she'll shut down. I'm a bastard, but part of me is relieved she has to stay here until Ron tells her it's okay to leave.

"I'm fine. I don't know what you're talking about." She looks annoyed, and takes a large swallow of her coffee, grimacing as the still too hot liquid burns on the way down.

"Bree." I put my coffee mug down, and reach my hand across to grab hers. "You remind me of someone, someone very important to me, someone I love…loved…more than anyone else in this world." I feel an uncharacteristic lump in my throat. I don't usually cry when talking about my mom, but somehow bringing her up like this, talking to Bree about her, makes it all feel so much more intimate. "She had a horrible life, my mom…" I exhale sharply before continuing. "My dad, he was a bastard. He made her life, and our lives, mine and Jake's, well, he made all of our lives hell on earth." Bree lowers the mug from her face and gives me her entire focus.

"She was sad, like you, towards the end. She didn't see an end in sight. She failed to protect my brother and me." Bree pulls her hand from mine, and I see her open her mouth to protest, but I continue cutting her off. "I know that's the wrong thing to say, I know I should say something about her being perfect, but she wasn't. She married an asshole, and gave him two sons. She didn't leave; she never tried. I'm okay with it, I forgive her for that, but it doesn't change it. She did try to protect us in her own way, and I know that she did save my ass more than once. But, in the end, my father won because he defeated her. He almost took Jake and I down with the ship, too." Bree is looking at me with her hands in her lap, from the way her arms are flexing I think she's got her hands clasped together and is squeezing them. I take a deep breath, finalizing my decision to share this part of me with her.

"When I came home that day, about 10 years ago, I knew something was wrong as soon as I walked in the house. Everything was too quiet." I take another deep breath.

"Mom always met me at the door, and gave me some sort of indication as to what kind of mood dad was in. If he was in a good mood, she would greet me with a small smile. I don't think she had fully smiled in years. A bad mood meant she would give me a hug and usually whisper some kind of warning about where and how he was …like 'Stay out of the living room,' or 'Just go straight to your room.' If we were lucky, and he was at work, she would just call out from wherever she was in the house, usually the kitchen." I give Bree a weak smile before I continue talking.

"Mom really did help us in her own way, like I said before. She was the one that bought me a deadbolt for my bedroom door. See, my Dad liked to come into my room at night and take his anger out on me. I was his own personal punching bag for fucking years. But it was nothing compared to what he did to Jake. That's a different conversation though, a story that only Jake can have." Bree's eyes widen, probably understanding my meaning as she nods in agreement.

"Anyway, the deadbolt had worked for a while, until Dad finally lost his shit and kicked my door down. She also ended up helping me go from dump to dump until we found a door that would work as a replacement. I always tried to focus on the good more than the bad. The reality was… is… at times… too hard to swallow. My mom was ultimately a woman who had stayed with an abuser, and allowed her children to be abused. It's not easy to understand that and forgive her, but I loved her enough to try and, most days, I think I'm there." Now comes the hard part. I open my hand on the cushion between us, palm up, and Bree grabs my hand with no hesitation.

"That day, nothing but silence greeted me when I got home. I called out, looking for Mom, and making my way toward the kitchen, walking softly. Mom always stayed in the kitchen, or the backside of the house, even when she wasn't cooking. It was her subtle way of avoiding being where my father was, by faking being busy with random shit. I knew she hadn't gone anywhere. She wasn't allowed to leave the house without Dad very often." I clench my eyes closed before I open my mouth to speak again.

"When I rounded the corner into the kitchen, I found her. She was there." My voice cracks. "In the kitchen." I open my eyes, now full of tears, and see Bree looking at me intently, her eyes mirroring mine.

"I knew she was dead the minute I saw her, but I still ran up to her and grabbed her cold wrist. I shouted her name a few times. Her eyes were open, and staring out the kitchen window. I knew she sat there sometimes, and just stared off into the distance. I always figured she was dreaming about a different life, a better life, a life without my father. Because that situation wasn't already fucked up enough, as soon as I found her, I heard the front door opening. I called out a greeting. I can't remember what I said. I was just hoping against all odds it was Jake. I knew my dad wouldn't be able to handle my mom's death. It wasn't that he really cared about her, but the fact that he wasn't in control of her anymore, that she had escaped him in the end, that would push him over any edge he had left. I also knew who would pay the price for his rage." I take another shuddering breath and glance at Bree. She's still gripping my hand, and completely focused on me.

"I remember my father yelling something about being hungry. He had no idea what was going on, he was too selfish to see anything but himself, and I heard his heavy footsteps moving towards where I was in the kitchen. I knew in that moment I wasn't helpless anymore. I could fight back now. Jake wasn't home, and there was nothing else my father could use against me, not with mom gone. I closed my eyes and tried to focus. I knew everything was about to change. None of our lives were going to be the same after that day. So, I ignored the tears in my eyes and took one last look at mom's face, trying to memorize it. She looked beautiful." I give Bree another weak smile. "She looked peaceful. I told her I loved her, and that she was free now. Then, I stood up to my full height and braced for what was about to happen. I knew these last few seconds were the calm before the storm."

Bree's breathing hitches as a single tear falls down her cheek.

"What happened?" Bree asks, giving my hand a reassuring squeeze. The fact that despite being raped less than 24 hours ago, that she would want to comfort me, blows my mind. She's so much stronger than she gives herself credit for.

"My dad walked into the kitchen, and took one look at me standing next to the... her body. He screamed at me and then, the next thing I knew, I woke up in a hospital two days later. I never saw him again after that." That last part isn't a complete lie, I'm just leaving quite a bit out. I can't tell her anything else. I gave my word to Jake, and it's his story to tell.

Bree's eyes are full of tears as she squeezes my hand again. The silence that follows the end of my story isn't awkward. We both retreat to the safety of our own minds before I end the moment by deciding I need more coffee and getting up. Coffee is a priority. Always.

"Thank..." Bree's voice cuts off, and she clears her throat. "Thank you for sharing that with me. It can't be easy to talk about something like that. I can't even imagine." She shyly meets my gaze, as I lower myself back down to sit next to her.

"At first, it was hard to talk about, really hard. But I refused to feel ashamed of what happened. My mother didn't make a choice that many people would agree with. I don't agree with it, but it was her choice to make. I love my mom. She was the only parent I had, in my opinion. But there were... things... that happened. Things that people shouldn't have to live through, but we did. I guess it was just too much for her." I take a deep breath as the thoughts I've struggled with my whole life come to the forefront again. Was she a coward for killing herself? Was she a failure as a mother because she never left my father, because she didn't protect Jake or me? God, poor Jake. He had it so much worse than I did.

Bree must catch on to my declining mood because she's quick to change the subject.

"It's okay. Let's talk about something else." Bree sets her half empty coffee mug on the table. It's one of my favorites. It says "Have a nice day", but has a middle finger carved into the bottom. I don't think she realizes she's been flipping me off every time she took a sip. She looks around my sparse apartment, and I can see her brain working on trying to find a better topic.

"How long have you lived here?" She's at least subtle in questioning why everything is so bare.

"About a year. I moved around a lot whenever I got restless before I decided I wanted to settle near Jake. To make some place my home."

"What did you do for work if you travelled so much?" Bree asks, and then almost looks like she regrets it. She's probably assuming I've done work similar to Jake's and Ron's.

I answer quickly to make her feel comfortable. "Bartending is an easy job to find. I've travelled all over the country, and a few places in Europe, just going where the wind takes me." I lean back, crossing my legs so my right ankle rests on top of my left knee.

"Where did you live in Europe?" I can tell this is something Bree really finds interesting because she leans forward unconsciously, bringing her knee close enough to my thigh, I can feel her body heat.

"London. I took a train somewhere different every time I had a few days off. I managed to see Paris several times, and then I spent a week in Germany. A small town near Hannover, friendliest people I've ever met. Had a good friend there named Mika. I promised him I would come back some time to visit. I really should. They have the best fucking beer."

Watching her face as she listens to me intently, I want to touch her. I feel like such a bastard, but I want her, and not just physically. I want *her*. I want to know what's going on in her head. I want to know why she's so sad, why she thinks she deserved what happened last night. She hasn't said that, but her attitude about it was pretty obvious. *Be patient,* I remind myself. I've never really wanted a girl for the long haul, but, after such a short time with Bree, I'm determined she is going to be that girl. She's going to be mine. Thankfully, before I can make an ass out of myself, my phone rings. I run to the kitchen, where I left it charging last night, and see that it's Jake.

"Sup?" I answer the phone, wondering if I should go back to Bree or stay here. There's a pretty good chance there will be parts of this conversation she doesn't need to overhear.

"It's done," Jake says ominously.

I snort out a laugh before I can catch myself. "What are we, in a Godfather movie? What the fuck does that even mean?"

"That means that the motherfucker is dead. Ron killed him personally. He kept mouthing off, said she liked it, said girls like her don't matter. They're only good for one thing. Greg ended up pulling me off of him but... fucking hell. I'm telling you I've never seen Ron go off like that. I've seen him be nicer to guys that straight up stole from him. I'll be honest, man. I've never seen something so cold blooded in my life. Ron went fuckin' crazy."

Shit fuck. I don't know what Bree's understanding with Ron was, but I know her enough to know this isn't going to sit well with her. I also know she's going to blame herself for this. I won't lie and say I don't get a sick satisfaction out of knowing the asshole that put his hands on Bree is gone. He will never hurt her again.

"You gonna be okay?" I ask, afraid of the answer.

"Yeah, man, you know Ron has us covered with the pigs." Jake makes a snorting noise, and I hear Greg laugh in the background.

"I wasn't talking about the cops." I lower my voice. I don't know how much Bree can hear, but this apartment is small as hell.

"Yeah, I am. I know you always associate violence with dad, but sometimes it's necessary. Sometimes, it's what you have to do. Am I happy we took this asshole out? Yes, yes the fuck I am." Greg's laughter in the background stops, and Jake lets out a deep sigh. I know the burden he carries more than anyone else; I know his lifestyle takes a toll on him.

"It will be okay, Jake. You know that. We got this. Together… always," Greg says in a quiet voice, but I can still hear him in the background. Something about the comment strikes me as intimate, too intimate for two thugs working together, but I let it go. I have enough shit on my plate right now.

"Keep me posted," I say, trying to end the call and get back to Bree.

"How is she?" Jake asks, oblivious to my intentions. I can hear wind in the background, and know he must be driving somewhere. Getting Jake off the phone when he's driving is damn near impossible.

"I don't know. She's acting fine, but I know better. We know better." I run my fingers through my hair, and cringe when they get stuck. I probably look like I have a rat's nest on my head right now.

"Yeah, we do." Jake pauses and takes a deep breath. "We're at my place. Text me if she needs anything." Jake hangs up before giving me a chance to respond. I know that Jake, more than anyone, can understand Bree's situation, but I selfishly hope I don't need to call him for help.

Despite my protests, Bree insists on leaving for her own apartment. Ron calls Bree before she leaves and tells her in no uncertain terms that he doesn't want to see her at work for at least another few days. I can tell by her eyes that Bree doesn't like this, but she simply hangs up the phone, and silently walks out of my apartment, refusing my offer to walk her home.

Chapter 8

Bree

I wish I'd never been born. That's the closest way I can describe how I feel right now. It's been a few long, painful days since Nate attacked me. I managed to escape Declan's apartment, and neither he nor Ron were crazy about me going home, but I needed my own space. I've returned to work, but Ron has now instituted two nights off a week for me. I'm not happy about it.

Now, I'm sitting in my bathtub, smoking a cigarette and staring at a half empty bottle of vodka. I don't know why I'm here anymore. I don't know how to exist in this world. I've seen too much of the ugly. In all the pretty faces, I see nothing but lies and fake relationships. Everyone who has ever claimed to love me was lying. I've tried for so long to exist anyway and I just can't do it.

I've spent years of my life pretending to be okay. Pretending I'm the same as everyone around me. I'll never be satisfied with face value wisdom and happy lies. I've spent my entire life striving to just be alive. I'm incapable of being satisfied with that. The weight of my pain, my damage, suffocates me. I can't relate. I can't understand. When you've literally had to fight for your next breath against someone who claims to love you, against someone that swore to protect you, how can I then possibly care about my loneliness? I don't have it in me anymore. I have maybe a few friendships, if you could even call them that. People like Ron. Our relationship remains mostly because of who *he* is, not because of who *I* am. For years, this has been okay. I was born to always come in second, but second place is just first loser, isn't it? I give a weak chuckle to that thought, and then sigh in frustration. I'm so very tired of this.

I take another drag from my cigarette and grab the vodka bottle, pulling it to my lips. I don't even notice the burn anymore as it runs down my throat. I wonder how much vodka I have to drink to not wake up again? Could I just fall asleep in the tub, and not wake up tomorrow to more pain? I lean back against the edge of the tub and close my eyes. The room is silent, just the subtle sound of the heat blowing through the vent, and the occasional sound of the water moving around me. I open my eyes and stare at the off-white ceiling. I count the times the fluorescent light flickers.

It flickers fifteen times before I take another large swallow of vodka.

It flickers twenty this time before I bring the bottle to my lips again.

I begin to feel heavy. My hand moves in a sluggish way trying to balance the vodka bottle on the side of the tub. It falls over the side and, from the sound of it, shatters. Just fucking great.

I decide to ignore that problem as well and slink lower into the water and close my eyes.

And just when I make my mind up, just when I hit rock bottom, a glimmer of hope appears out of nowhere. I see Declan's face in my mind. I know he is probably just like every other bastard in my life, but there is something about him. Like he believes in me. Like he knows more about me than I do. I think of everything he went through. Everything he hinted at Jake going through. Surely, if they can survive that, I can survive this, right? That small glimmer is all it takes, and I feel hope coming from inside me, almost against my will. This is both my blessing and my curse.

My eyes open in frustration, my hands clench suddenly and tightly, causing the water to slosh around them. Why can't I be allowed to give up? Why can't I have a reprieve? But there is always something there in between, a far off place where I am loved. I don't have to try to understand rules to these invisible mind games. I am me, and not being punished for it doesn't seem fathomable to me. I should stay in the moment, stay in my darkness but instead, I find myself searching for this place of beauty in my mind.

The pain in my heart is a physical pain, but it's a different kind of pain. It's the hopeful kind. The kind that says this is going to hurt but it's worth it. I want more than anything to become that little girl again, with nothing but a bright future ahead of me. I sob, the sound echoing off the tiled walls, using the back of my hand to wipe the tears from my face, and my shoulders shake.

Could I ever become untouched by the agony of life? Could the hole in my heart ever be full? The feeling leaves almost as quickly as it comes. As much as I try to, I can't hold on to this hopeful place; it's always just out of reach, giving me a small piece of heaven in between my moments of pain. This is why I'm still alive. The something there in between will never let me end this, emerging when I need it the most, then vanishing as quickly as it arrives.

I stub my cigarette out in the ashtray on the side of the tub, and lean back, submerging my body so that only my face is sticking out from the lukewarm water. I'm so exhausted. The weight of life is too much for me to carry most days. I'm tired of being so disenchanted. Just once, I would like for someone to actually be who he or she said they were.

There really isn't a way to properly explain the pain of having a parent reject you...your *only* parent reject you. It's so far from the realm of "normal" it's like the earth getting knocked off its axis. It sets a standard in your mind. It sets expectations. In your entire life, there are two people that are supposed to always be safe.

Something There In Between

Two people whose love should be unconditional. My father died right after I was born, and my mother has made it clear I was nothing to her but dirt on the bottom of her shoe. As a little girl, I took my mother's rejection personally, because it was. It is. I took the weight of her failure on my little shoulders. It was my fault. It is my fault. Her hate had to be because of me. I watched her love everyone else in her life. I watched my friends thrive in an environment I couldn't even comprehend. I've never even had a hug from my mother that wasn't forced by some sense of social obligation. I only remember her saying she loved me once. She gave me a lecture and managed to spit out that she "didn't like me, but she loved me because she had to." I remember her hugging me, almost in glee, after telling me no one else wanted me. I was a blight, a burden to her and her precious life. I remember her making sure all good things were celebrated without my presence; I was never included. I was always an afterthought. I was just a child… a frightened, small, vulnerable child.

I pretended I was tough when I ran away with Alex. The reality is, I was, and I am, so broken, so frail. I just needed someone to show me what love was. I needed someone to fight for me, to show me that I was worth something, anything. I still feel like I'm waiting for this some days. As time goes on, I learn more and more, that no one else is going to save me. Every moment I look out for myself is a reminder no one else is going to. I can't move on, and I can't get over it, no matter how hard I try. I can't pretend there isn't a raw, festering wound where my heart should be. All these thoughts are consuming. If I could have just one day without this pain, without this hurt…such a sweet relief that would be.

I know I can't just end this. No matter how much vodka I drink, no matter how much lower I let my body sink in the bath tub, I know I can't end this, but *God* do I want to.

I decide it's time to break my self-imposed solitude. It's too cold to sit on my bench and for the first time in a long while, I actually feel like being around people. I dress comfortably in my standard black jeans, heavy biker boots, my beanie hat, and my dark green military jacket. It's so cold these nights.

When I exit my building, and begin walking towards Keegan's, I almost stop and turn back around more than once. *If you're going to be miserable and drunk, at least do it around other people.* I repeat this, adopting it as a warped mantra until I round the corner to Keegan's and see a few random people standing outside smoking. I push past them, nodding slightly in acknowledgement of the few that toss out a greeting.

Opening the door to the bar, I'm overwhelmed by the scent of beer and stale cigarettes. Despite Ron discouraging smoking inside, beginning two years ago, the smell lingers. No one listens.

Something There In Between

I see a few startled faces look up when I make my way to the bar. I'm aware I'm being watched, and take a moment to be grateful I'm no longer limping. I sit on a bar stool, and rap my knuckles on the bar to get Declan's attention. It's a total waste of time, though; he was already watching me like a hawk from the moment I walked in.

"What's your poison?" Declan asks in an exaggerated southern accent. He leans down on his forearms, his hands mere centimeters from mine.

Suddenly, I wonder what would happen if I just grabbed his hands and held on. Would he let me? Would he laugh it off and push me away? Would he know just how much something so small would mean to me? I brush my thoughts aside, and look back up to Declan's face. His brows are furrowed, and I know he's reading me like an open book. I don't know how he does that.

"I'll have a vodka tonic, please." I don't bother returning his playful accent.

"How many have you had already?" he asks, raising an eyebrow at me and shooting a sideways glance in the direction of Ron's office. My gaze follows his, and I see Ron standing in the doorway, looking at me. I give him a weak smile, and he nods his head, more at Declan than me. I should be mad Declan had to ask for permission before serving me, but I don't have the energy to care. It's taking everything I have to follow through with my plan to be at the bar.

"I'm about get off if you want me to walk you home," Declan offers as he sets what is clearly a weak vodka tonic in front of me.

"Nah, I'm good. I'll have this and hang out for a while maybe," I mumble, raising the straw to my mouth. It might be my imagination, but I swear Declan's eyes darken slightly, as I pull the straw between my lips and pull the cold liquid into my mouth.

"Well, we're closing soon. You shouldn't have waited so long to come out." Declan is half teasing I can tell, but part of me feels a little self-conscious by his statement. I didn't even check the time when I got dressed and came out. Staying locked inside my apartment for the last twelve hours, and the days I was healing, has made me lose all sense of time and direction. I glance at the clock behind the bar, and realize it's almost 1 am. I lost an entire day and had no idea.

"Oh, I guess I haven't been keeping track of time since I've been at home resting," I say in an almost sarcastic tone. It's been anything but restful staring at the four walls of my prison.

"I gotta sleep since I have to be in here again tomorrow. You sure you don't want me to walk you home?" Declan asks before looking towards Ron's door again. This time it's closed and Ron is nowhere to be seen.

Something There In Between

I shake my head no, and Declan raps his knuckles on the bar a few times before he walks away to go home. I pretend I don't see the disappointment in his eyes. I suck the rest of my drink down as I swivel on my stool to follow him with my eyes. As I watch Declan walk towards the door, it's pretty clear he's dragging his feet, walking so much slower than normal. He hesitates by the door and for a brief second, I wonder if he's thinking about me, if he's going to come back towards me. It definitely seems like he's about to look for me behind him, but of course, that would be ridiculous. He has an entire life that doesn't involve me. Why on earth would he be thinking about me?

"Because you're an idiot and hope he is," I whisper to myself.

"You're not ready for that," Ron's voice interrupts my pity party, and startles me so much that I jump slightly, sloshing the liquid in my half empty glass. He must have snuck right up to me. He's standing right beside me, leaning on the bar. I look at him, and tilt my head in an unspoken question.

"You're not ready for that," he repeats himself as he slides a business card across the bar top towards me. "But you are ready for this. Call him tomorrow."

I pick up the card and look it over:

Ze BARROS
Fitness and Self Defense
3436 Lockridge Dr

678-555-3405

"I need to get in shape?" I ask in confusion.

"Yeah, inside and out," Ron says mysteriously, before he starts to reach his hand out to me, but he seems to change his mind and he just walks off. I stare after him, not understanding at all. But if Ron wants me to call, I will call. I need this job and my apartment. My life isn't great, but it would be a hell of a lot worse without those two things.

Chapter 9

Declan

The next few days of working at Keegan's fly by. It's a slow Wednesday night in the bar, but the calm is appreciated. Bree is finally back at work, in somewhat of a normal routine, though she has more days off a week now per Ron's orders. Tonight, she's mostly just sitting on a stool near the register, and I'm glad to be able to keep an eye on her. It's nowhere near as much as I would like, but pretty close. The first big meeting between Ron and the New York outfit is soon, and I can only imagine what kind of madness that is going to be. I've never been around one of Ron's meetings before, but I have heard plenty of stories from Jake. Granted half of what he said was probably bullshit; the other half was still pretty wild.

I wish I could say I had more breakthroughs with Bree, but she's been pretty shut down since the night I watched her at the park and when she was at my apartment. Her cheek and lip are healing nicely, and her limp is gone now. During my time here, we seem to have fallen into a nice routine.

She hasn't smiled any more, but she definitely seems less annoyed with my presence. I try to talk to her, but usually I can't get more than a nod or a one-word response. I can't explain it, but I feel more and more drawn to her, despite her clearly not being interested. She doesn't know it yet, but I'm going to be part of her life. A much bigger part than the coworker role she seems to have slipped me into.

As if sensing that I'm thinking about her, she looks up from where she's collecting empty glasses and wiping a table down. I meet her gaze and waggle my eyebrows in a lecherous way. That corner of her mouth lifts up and she shakes her head. I'm just opening my mouth to say something when the front door bursts open. The bang of the heavy doors hitting the walls beside them, echoes through the mostly calm and quiet room, a gush of cold air following in its wake.

"DEC! Get your bitch ass over here!" Jake roars. *I love my brother, I really do.* I repeat this to myself as I make my way towards him and the group with him. Jake is clearly drunk and the guys he came in with, including Greg, don't seem to be any better off.

"Dec, you've been here for a while now and we have to properly welcome you to the family," Jake says, his eyes full of glee, and I'm slightly terrified. Jake is a balls to the wall kind of guy, not much middle ground. His idea of celebrating could be anything from burning down a building, to getting so drunk we can't move for a few days, or possibly some combination of the two. Of course, he's already pretty close to that last one already.

"Okayyy…" I draw the word out, trying to not act as nervous as I feel. Jake is like an animal; he smells fear.

"Dec meet, um…" He looks to his right, and I see a small woman tucked under his arm. She's wearing a jean skirt that is so short, it can best be described as vagina length. Her tits are huge, obviously fake, and about to fall out of the tank top she's wearing, which is sporting the Keegan's logo. She has got to be freezing her ass off. She's wearing a shit ton of makeup, but I can tell she's cute, if you're into that sort of thing. When she realizes Jake is waiting for her to supply her name, I see annoyance flash in her eyes before she looks at me, then they light up. I see something lurking in them, though. Calculation? Whatever it is, my spidey senses begin to tingle.

"Candice, my name is Candice," she purrs, extending her hand to me.

I can already tell where this is heading, and I don't like it. However, I technically do owe my brother for this job, and keeping this job means being in good with him and the guys who are obviously a part of this… celebration. Rejecting his and by association, Ron's welcome aboard gift, would be beyond insulting.

I frantically search my brain, but I can't find a legitimate excuse to get out of this. So, I bite the bullet and give her a handshake. As soon as her small hand is in my larger one, Jake pushes her toward me, all but slamming her body up against mine.

"You're a big boy, aren't you?" she purrs, wrapping her free hand around my waist, and rubbing her tits against my side.

Despite my lack of interest, I am in fact a red-blooded, straight male, and boobs are kind of cool, so I feel myself hardening in my jeans. Candice must feel it, too, because she lets out a giggle. I think it's supposed to be cute, but it comes across as obnoxious. She lowers her hand and cups my half hard dick through the denim. I shoot Jake a panicked glance.

"Here, fucker." Jake shoves a bottle of whiskey into my free hand and mouths, *You're welcome.*

Realizing there really isn't anything I can do to get out of this, and remembering the fact that it's been more than a hot minute since I got any, I decide to roll with it. Taking a swig of my bottle, I let go of Candice's hand, squeezing my arm out from between us, and reach around her to cup her ass. I have to damn near bend in half, which puts my neck in range of her mouth. She starts licking me. Usually my neck is one of my more erogenous zones, but who just starts licking someone with no preamble? I take another swig, and this becomes my default when Candice does something I don't like or understand for the next couple of hours. Drink after drink slips down my throat until I don't even notice the burn anymore.

Something There In Between

Before I know it, I've been partying with Jake and the guys for a couple of hours and I'm wasted, wasted being an understatement. I know I finished the bottle Jake put in my hand, but I don't remember it being replaced. I know Ron stopped by our group, slapping me on the back and giving me a welcome speech, before instructing Candice to be sure "you make the boy happy."

I vaguely remember some shots and other drinks, but I'm definitely holding a half empty bottle of vodka right now, and I have no idea if I'm the reason its half gone or not. I'm standing, leaning against the wall, facing a table full of Greg, Quinn and a few other guys, whose names I can't remember.

Jake is entertaining everyone with his spectacular dance moves to the right. Dancing has always been the sign that it's time to take Jake home. When the dance moves come out, it's time to roll out. We had coined that phrase after a disastrous weekend trip to Vegas.

Candice is literally glued to my side. If she got any closer, I think she would have to actually crawl inside my ass. Bree is noticeably absent. I know she's still here working, but I haven't seen her since Jake dragged me over here. If I'm being honest, I've avoided looking for her. Part of me is very ashamed that she's seeing this or that I'm even doing this. Either one. Deciding it's time to break the seal, I gently push Candice off my body and walk to the bathroom.

I finish my business, and start washing my hands, when I hear the bathroom door open.

"I think I'm done for the night, man," I say, as I turn expecting to see Jake or one of the guys but instead, see Candice shutting the door behind her. I hear the telltale click of the lock, and she starts walking towards me. She's shaking her hips in such an exaggerated way, I think I'm supposed to find it sexy, but she's shaking her hips so hard I'm tempted to ask her if she's having some sort of seizure. My ADD brain is snapped back into focus when I feel hands on the waistband of my jeans.

"But, baby, we're not done yet," she murmurs before sinking to her knees in front of me. She looks up to my face and licks her lips. She has lipstick on her teeth, and I debate if now is the right moment to tell her that or not. Before I can open my mouth, she nuzzles the crotch of my jeans.

Clearly, I'm not as drunk as I thought because my dick immediately springs to life. It's almost painful, as all the blood in my body runs to one place. She licks her lips again, and pulls the zipper down on my fly after undoing the button. I'm usually a commando guy, and probably should have warned her or something. Next thing I know, my cock springs free and, with a loud smacking sound, hits her in the eye.

"Jesus," she whines letting go of my jeans, and sitting back on her heels while covering her eye. "What the fuck was that?

That was too hard to have just been your dick," she says, rubbing her eye and looking at me.

My jeans are sagging down my thighs, my cock and balls swinging free. Well, pointing free? I don't know what the right term is. I do know the minute she sees my piercing because her eyes grow wide, and an almost evil smile crosses her face.

"Oh, baby, I'm gonna have fun with that," she purrs, reaching for my dick and stroking me from base to tip. She lets her thumb slide over my Prince Albert piercing that just smacked her in the face, and I can't help the moan that comes from my mouth.

"Such a big boy," she croons, leaning forward and licking the tip. My head rolls back, and smacks the wall. I don't remember moving to lean against the wall, but I am very grateful for the extra support. I close my eyes as my dick is engulfed in warm, wet heat. It's almost disturbing how good Candice is at this. Then suddenly, Bree's face pops into my head. I open my eyes and look around the room. Candice and I are still alone, and she's going down on me like her life depends on it. I'm not a small guy, and she's all but swallowing my whole cock down her throat. It's been so long and it feels *so* good. I close my eyes again. Blue eyes are staring back, that radiant smile, and suddenly, I realize I'm about to come. I open my eyes again, and gently push on Candice's shoulders until she releases my dick with a popping sound.

"Grab onto the sink and bend over," I order, reaching into my back pocket to grab my wallet. Once it's out, I yank a condom from my billfold and tear the foil packet open with my teeth. Candice obeys me, grabbing the sink and bending damn near in half. Her barely there skirt lifts up, showing me a smooth ass and shaved pussy. Damn, she wasn't even wearing underwear under that tiny thing?

After sheathing myself, I walk up behind her and take myself in hand. Once we're lined up, I thrust in, hard and deep. Candice's feet rise off the floor with the force of my thrust, her grip on the sink so tight her knuckles are white. She squeals and then moans as I slowly pull out. I set up a rhythm, slamming into her quickly, then pulling out slowly. After a few minutes, Candice is squealing so loud it's hurting my ears, so I bend over her and wrap one hand around her mouth. The other grabs onto her shoulder and I start pumping into her so hard it feels like we might go through the wall. The sink is creaking with the weight of us slamming into it so hard. I wonder how mad Ron would be if I destroy his bathroom? I can't find it in me to care right now. Even with my hand covering her mouth, she's loud as fuck. I feel the familiar tightening in my balls, and my thrusting becomes faster and faster.

Something There In Between

Candice suddenly lets out a deep moan, and I feel her pussy clamp down on me. That's all it takes, and my eyes roll back in my head as I fill the condom.

I choose to not acknowledge the fact that, yet again, Bree's face was all I saw when I closed my eyes. I thrust weakly for another minute or two trying to prolong our pleasure, but making sure my eyes stay open before grabbing the end of the condom. I carefully pull out, turn around to remove it, and then toss it away. Candice slowly stands up and pushes her skirt back down. Honestly, I don't know why she even bothers. Now that my orgasm is over, I realize I'm fucking exhausted. I slowly fix my pants, and wash my hands in the sink again.

"Baby, that was so good," Candice says, coming up behind me and wrapping her arms around me. I stiffen, but then ask myself why. Why am I so against this? I just fucked her in a bathroom. Clearly, this girl isn't after a relationship, something I'm not interested in, but if she wants to go another round, why the fuck not? Bree's face flashes through my mind again, and I shake both the image, and the guilt it brings, away.

"You're coming home with me." It's not a question, more of a command, and Candice nods her agreement as I take her hand and open the bathroom door. As soon as the door opens, there is a thunderous applause from the guys still hanging around. If I were a better person, I would have felt embarrassed, but I have no shame so I give a little bow and smack Candice on her ass for good measure.

"Jake, I'm out," I say, heading toward the door. Candice is stumbling behind me in her heels. I probably should slow down since my legs are much longer than hers, but I can't find it in me to care.

"Wrap that shit up. Twice!" Jake calls behind me, such a fucking gentleman.

I shake my head and open the door to the street when, for some reason, the urge hits me to look back. I stop halfway through the door, my head lowered and slightly turned toward the bar. *Don't do it, Dec,* I say to myself as I start to turn my head and then stop. I don't know why my mind wants me to look back at Bree, but it's a horrible idea. I refuse to think about why she's on my mind at this exact moment, and decide to drown myself in Candice's pussy and more booze. With that decision made, I turn my head without looking back, and march out of the door like a man on a mission.

Chapter 10

Bree

Things settle down quickly after Declan left with the girl, and Jake stopped his ridiculous dance moves. It's becoming more of an effort to not laugh around Declan and Jake. Declan definitely brings out the fun side of Jake and, well, pretty much everything.

After closing up the bar, I start my lonely walk home. All the distractions from the night are gone, and I'm alone with my thoughts once again. My chest physically hurts, as all the grief slams back into me.

For some reason the image of Declan walking out with the blonde woman plays over and over again in my head. It's quickly followed by the image of Alex walking away with his mystery girl. Yes, thank you, head, I get it. Everyone is walking away from me with a better option.

Pulling my earbuds out of my purse, I queue up my 'emotional' playlist and trudge along. The air is getting colder and colder, and more leaves are on the ground. I wrap my arms around myself, letting the melody flow over me. Soon, it will be too cold to sit in the park at night. I shudder, this time not from the cold, but at the thought of having no way to escape the suffocating apartment. Winter is so hard on me for this reason. It also reminds me of when Alex left. A few days from now, it will be the anniversary of the day he didn't show up. The day he was supposed to come home, but didn't.

I shiver on my bench, wishing I could just let go of this pain. How can I want to get rid of something so badly, but still cling to it so strongly? I have to find the balance between not being consumed by my past, but at the same time I can't let myself forget it. I have to remember, so it doesn't happen again. Never again will I be fooled into thinking I'm loved. Never again will I share myself with anyone. I know I'm not good enough for either of those things. My existence is lonely, but the pain is tolerable. I repeat that lie over and over again in my head until I can almost believe it.

Once I give up on sitting on the bench, and make it inside to the warmth of the apartment, I crawl into bed and my mind wanders back to Declan. I wonder if he's still with that girl. He was really drunk. Did he manage to stay awake long enough to fuck her again? Or did he just pass out? More importantly, why is that last thought making me feel something eerily close to hope in my chest? I jump out of bed and take a double dose of sleeping medication, chasing it with a shot of liquor. I need to not think anymore tonight.

The next morning, I make a point to wake up at ten in the morning, which is early in bartender time, and call the number on the card Ron gave me when I went into Keegan's on my own.

"Hello," a lightly accented male voice answers after the second ring.

"Um, yeah, hi… this is Bree, Ron gave me your card?" I stutter, my confidence leaving me. I still have no idea why I'm calling this Ze guy or whoever he is.

"Bree, I'm so glad you called." He greets me like he's been expecting me to call. "Tell me what time you want to get together, I have an opening today at 1:00 pm if you can make it?" His tone is almost fatherly, and something about him makes me feel comfortable. I immediately feel myself relax.

I glance at the clock reflexively. "Yes, I can do one. What should I wear?"

"Something you can work out and move freely in. See you at one." He hangs up without another word, and I stare at my phone in shock for a minute.

I take a quick shower, and decide to head out early. This way, my nerves won't get the best of me. My body may be healing but my mind is fucked. Anything I can do to stay calm helps. The city buses are more crowded and more unreliable the colder the weather gets and something tells me Ze will not be happy if I'm late. I lace up my neglected running shoes and braid my hair quickly. I exit my building, and pull on one of Alex's old skateboarding sweatshirts, pulling the hood over my head as the cold breeze does its best to blow me over when I reach the sidewalk.

During the entire bus ride, and walk to the address on the card, I become increasingly nervous. This isn't a great part of the city; the buildings go from looking old, to poorly maintained, to flat out abandoned. Trash litters the streets and graffiti decorates the walls lining the street. I have no doubt that, when the weather is warmer, there are homeless people on every corner here. I make a mental note to see about bringing some old blankets and sweatshirts out here. Winter is brutal when you have nowhere to go. I should know. I shake my head, and send up a silent thank you that this is no longer my reality.

At 12:55 pm sharp, I am standing outside what looks like an abandoned warehouse. The parking lot has been repaved, and is half full with newer looking cars, which is reassuring. Obviously, there has to be some sort of business inside of it. The building however, looks like it should be condemned. One more gust of this freezing wind and the building will probably fall over. I walk up to the door, and raise my hand to open it, but the door is pulled open from the inside before my hand reaches it. An older man is standing in the doorway. He isn't much taller than me, but has broad shoulders and is obviously in excellent shape. His jet-black hair has grey liberally sprinkled through it, and he's wearing a black t-shirt over a pair of black athletic pants. His dark brown eyes look over my face, assessing me, and I immediately know we're going to get along.

"Bree?" he asks. "I'm Ze."

"That's me," I say lamely, and he opens the door all the way, beckoning me inside.

The inside of the building is the complete opposite of the outside. Bright lighting fills the huge space inside. The floors are some sort of light wood… bamboo, maybe? Definitely high quality. The right side of the room is full of regular gym equipment: treadmills, some free weights, and there is a bar running across the whole ceiling towards the back of the building, that has black and yellow straps hanging down from it. It almost looks like some sort of torture device. Ze follows my gaze.

"That's TRX. You'll get to that, but first we need to see where you're at physically," he says, looking me over. "No extra weight on you, but your muscle tone is shit. Do you exercise at all?" he asks, walking a full circle around me, and coming back to face me. I feel my cheeks heat under his critical gaze.

"No, I mean nothing besides walking a lot and whatever lifting is required at my job." All too familiar body issues seep into my brain. How many times in my life will I have to endure someone criticizing my body? I mean, honestly.

"What's that look mean?" he asks, leaning forward and squinting in my face.

"No…nothing," I stammer. Why can't this asshole just ignore my face like everyone else does? First Declan and now Ze. I must be losing my powers of invisibility.

"Look, I have one rule in this gym and that's total honesty. What is that look?" He holds my gaze, and I can't look away even though I want to. His eyes are unflinching; I know I have no choice but to answer him.

"I just– I guess I had been feeling better about my body lately, and you just kind of blew that out of the water." I feel my cheeks heating in a blush and, to my horror, tears building up in my eyes. I blink rapidly trying to push them back.

"I see Ron didn't exaggerate at all," Ze mutters, mostly to himself. "Let's go." He's walking off towards the treadmills before I can even open my mouth to ask him what he means. "Get on this, and we'll do a quick warm up to get your blood flowing. I'll take it easy on you today since you said you've not been working out regularly." He winks, and I know I'm fucked.

For the next forty-five minutes, I am subjected to what I'm fairly certain are CIA tactics to get enemies of the State to talk, all under the guise of a fitness test. I do pull ups, pushups, squats, lunges, leg presses and sit ups. I run a mile on the treadmill and survive two rounds of full minute planks. When it's over, I'm drenched in sweat and sitting on the floor with my knees against my chest and my arms wrapped around them.

"First, you need to stop that smoking shit." Ze hands me a bottle of water. I sip it gratefully, and give him a questioning look. I hadn't mentioned smoking at all. "You're what, twenty?" He doesn't give me time to answer before speaking again. "You're way too young to be heaving and breathing that hard. You're not even gonna be able to walk to the toilet without an inhaler if you keep that shit up." He gives me a stern look. "Other than that, you're not in horrible shape. We are going to make you stronger, and then we are going to make you faster." He leans in conspiratorially, before whispering, "We have the technology."

I think water comes out of my nose as I gasp and wheeze, laughing at his insanity. Ze gives me a sad smile. "When was the last time you laughed, kiddo?"

Tears well in my eyes and I purse my lips together, shaking my head. He leans forward and puts his hand on my shoulder. "You're the only one that can fix anything, but I can damn sure give you some tools to help." He gives my shoulder a squeeze. "OK, enough of the girl shit. Start running. I want 2 miles on the treadmill before I'll let you go home."

I give him a horrified look, but he just stands there expectantly. Wincing at my sore muscles, I rise to my feet slowly and make my way to the treadmill.

S. Ferguson

Chapter 11

Declan

My head feels like it was on fire, then someone stomped on it to put it out before they re-lit the fire. Seriously, I must be dying. This has to be Ebola. I lick my lips, trying to find some moisture left in my body. Based on the stale taste in my mouth, and how hot I feel, I must be in a desert somewhere, too. Cracking my eyes open as little as possible, I squint and look down the length of my body. I'm naked, which isn't too far out of the range of normal, but there is a tiny hand on my junk.

The fuck?

Tilting my head slightly to the right, and ignoring the dizziness it causes, I follow the arm the hand is attached to up to a slim shoulder. Raising my gaze high, I see a nest of bottle blonde hair resting right in my armpit. That can't feel or smell pleasant right now. As the fog clears, I realize Blondie has her entire body wrapped around me, and is holding my dick. I'm a little scared.

"Yo, wake up," I whisper, in case her head hurts as much as mine. I shift my body to the left, trying to ease out from under her, but her hand on my dick tightens and I freeze.

"Mmmmm, good morning, baby," she coos, sending a whiff of vile-smelling morning breath across my face. It takes me about two seconds to realize trying to stop the gagging is impossible, so I give up all pretense of gentleness, and lunge to my left away from her. I grimace when her nails scrape across my groin.

"What's wrong?" she shouts. Okay, it probably wasn't a shout, but it might as well have been with the hangover I'm suffering.

"Sick," I manage to grit out right before sliding into my bathroom and slamming the door shut.

Once I finish puking my fucking soul up, I brush my teeth, and decide to take a quick shower. Once I'm standing in the stream of hot water, I take inventory of my body. My back is burning, so I yank the shower curtain back, and look over my shoulder into the mirror on the cabinet. It looks like I got into a fight with a lion or a tiger. It looks like I lost. I am bleeding from some of the cuts. I see something on my neck, and turn around to face the mirror. I have two hickeys on my neck and one, no lie, two inches from my dick. What. In. The. Fuck.

I finish my shower pretty quickly, and wrap a towel around my waist, before walking out. Blondie is sitting up in my bed, the sheet draped across her waist, and her tits are hanging out. Her hair looks like something my neighbor's cat coughed up. Her makeup is smeared. She looks like she's trying out to be the next Alice Cooper with all the black eye liner smeared around her eyes and running down her cheeks.

"Sorry about that, I'm good now...." I let my words drop off. I have no idea who this chick is.

"Candice. I'm Candice. I can't believe you can't remember my name. You sure were screaming it last night," she says, giving me her best impression of a seductive look.

1) I literally have no idea what to say to that because:

2) I've had sex enough times in my life to know I'm not a screamer. I'm a dude.

3) I can't remember a goddamned thing from last night.

4) I've never had a one-night stand with someone that stayed the night. I always bailed before that could happen. I must have been completely obliterated to bring someone back to my apartment. I've had actual relationships with girls who never saw the inside of my apartment.

"Mind if I use your shower?" she asks, and I immediately feel relieved. Cool, she'll shower, then bail, and I can forget this ever happened once my back heals and I find a dermatologist that specializes in scarred tissue repair.

"Sure, I'll... um... I'll make some coffee," I mutter, walking to my dresser and pulling out a pair of gym shorts. I wait, thinking she'll be walking to the bathroom but she's still sitting there in all of her tits-out glory, staring at me like I'm a piece of chocolate. This has got to be the most awkward experience of my life. Finally, I say fuck it, and slip my shorts on under my towel.

She smirks at me and stands up, letting the sheet fall to the ground. Her body is noticeably absent of marks. Hmmmm. She shuts the bathroom door, and I all but run to my kitchen.

Coffee, this is a job for coffee.

My apartment is really small; I have a tiny-ass kitchen, which is connected to a tiny-ass living room that my tiny-ass bedroom door opens off of. The one and only bathroom is in my room, but as a single guy, it's not a big deal to me. Less space means less cleaning. When I open my bedroom door, my living room looks like a fucking bomb went off. Honestly, at this point, I'm not surprised. Pillows and cushions are thrown all over the place, and a lamp is knocked over. My coffee table is skewed and my one pride and joy, my huge flat screen TV, is on but the screen is blue. Thank God nothing got left on and burned into the screen overnight. I stumble through the wreckage, and find my beloved Keurig.

Once I have steaming coffee in my mug, my Darth Vader mug I might add, and way more than the recommended dosage of Motrin in my stomach, the world starts to make sense again. I stand in a thoughtful silence, leaning against my kitchen counter, and waiting for my unwanted guest to leave.

Blondie... Candice comes out of my room wearing one of my t-shirts. Not cool. She looks much better now that her hair is washed and combed, and all that makeup is gone from her face.

She's actually pretty. I wish I could remember what she looked like last night for comparison. She walks up to me, and wraps her arms around my middle, leaning her head into my chest. Okay, then...

"Thank you so much for last night. Jake told me his brother was a stud, but I had no idea. I'm gonna walk funny for a week," she says against my chest.

All I can think is *yeah me too,* wincing as my shirt rubs against the claw marks on my back.

"You're um, you're welcome. But I...uh..." Way to communicate, Dec. I take a centering breath, and look down at her face, as I slowly try to extract my body from her death grip. Seems like this chick is always holding onto me.

"Oh, you're one of those?" she says, standing back and putting her hands on her hips.

"And here we go," I mutter under my breath. I don't know if she hears me or not, but she assumes what can only best be described as the 'You're About to Get Your Ass Handed to You' stance. You know the one I'm talking about. It's when chicks put their hands on their hips, then cock one leg to the side, while they lean to that same side, giving you a look that could peel paint. If you're a straight dude, you've experienced this stance. Usually right before you—hey, you guessed it—get your ass handed to you.

"I know you weren't expecting to meet me and, to be honest, I wasn't expecting to meet you either, but I won't complain. Last night was unexpected and magical. I'll give you some time to process. I mean, I totally understand you needing some time. It's not every day you meet the person you're supposed to be with. I'll be here when you're ready, baby."

WHAT. THE. ACTUAL. FUCK. I repeat, *what the fuck?*

Alarm bells are going off in my head. Phrases like *Stage Five Clinger* and *Red Alert* are ricocheting around my head. My eyes widen, and I almost look around for Jake because this has to be some sort of prank. No way is Candice really that crazy. While I've been standing in a fear-induced stupor, Candice walks over to me and leans up on her toes to give my cheek a kiss. Apparently, my stunned silence is taken as agreement. Then, she grabs what I'm assuming is her purse from the carnage in my living room and prances out the door, wearing nothing but my t-shirt. My Teenage Mutant Ninja Turtles t-shirt, too. Motherfucker.

I decide I need to finish another cup of coffee before I even try to interpret what the fuck just happened and then I'll call Jake. Fortunately, he must have used his evil little brother senses to know I was thinking of him because my phone chose that exact moment to ring. After telling Bree the story of Jake's old nickname, I changed his ringtone to "Space Lord" by Monster Magnet. It's as close to acknowledging his Lord Pussy Magnet title as I will ever get, and it definitely makes me laugh every time I hear it play.

"So, did you survive Crazy Candice?" He's speaking before I've even raised my phone all the way to my ear.

"So, I take it the 'we're meant to be' speech wasn't a prank?" There is no disguising the hope in my voice.

"The fuck?" I hear Jake laughing so hard he's snorting. There is even laughter coming from around him, so he must have stayed above the bar last night. I stand stock still, clenching my jaw, while he and his friends continue to laugh at my expense.

"I'm glad I can be so amusing. What the fuck did you get me into, asshole?" I seethe, when I've decided I've had enough.

"Honestly, we all knew she was a little clingy but she's hot as hell. She's never pushed the bullshit that hard before. Usually, she just shows up where the guy she's fixated on works and calls his phone a bunch. You didn't give her your phone number, did you?" Jake is suddenly serious.

Fuck, did I? I still have no memory of last night, and I already broke my rules by bringing her here. "I don't know. Let me check." I switch Jake to speakerphone, and exit the call screen to look at my contacts. The background on my phone is a selfie of Candice. I cringe, and can already tell where this is heading. Sure enough, in my contacts list, the number one on my favorite's list, no less, is "WIFEY."

"I don't wanna talk about it," I mumble to Jake's guffaws. I hang up on him; I'm actually starting to be a legitimately scared now.

I toss my phone to the side, and rub both hands down my face. I absently notice my beard is longer than normal. Maybe it's time for a trim. I debate this for about five seconds and decide it's not worth the hassle. Despite my vicious hangover, I know a run is going to help cleanse my mind from all of Candice's crazy. I'll even pretend, when I run by a certain park, that it's an accident. That night, back at Keegan's, I make a futile attempt to talk to Bree about Ron. She's mostly healed now, but she's stonewalling my conversation in a way that would make the CIA proud.

Chapter 12

Bree

"Come on. Ron's like a father to you. You respect him." Declan turns slightly so he can see my face. He looks at me intently and again, I feel like he sees far more than he should. I quickly avert my gaze.

"I…" I stop speaking because I don't really know what to say. I never thought of Ron that way. Sure, he looks out for me, but I'm his employee. Obviously, he has to make sure I'm taken care of so I'll continue to work and keep my mouth shut about his business. Why would he care about what happened to me if I wasn't useful to him?

Declan continues to look at me, and when I risk a quick glance at him, his eyes look sad. He shuffles a little bit closer. Just those few inches make the moment feel far more intimate.

"You do know he cares about you, right?" he whispers, moving even closer to me.

I blink my eyes rapidly, not sure why I feel like crying. I don't wait for Declan to get any closer, so I just turn abruptly and flee to the ladies room. When I burst through the door, the tears are on the verge of escaping, and a few women who are standing in front of the mirror turn to look at me.

"Oh, honey, I hope you kicked his ass out. Don't put up with that shit," says an older woman with bright orange hair sympathetically, nodding toward my bruised cheek.

I just nod and keep my head down until the women make their way back out to the bar. I lean with both hands on the sink and close my eyes, lowering my head. How is it that I've been around the same people for years now but Declan, the guy I've known for such a short time, seems to see everything no one else does? I feel the panic rising in my chest. My self-preservation screams to avoid, to run, but I don't know how I can avoid Declan. We are working together for the foreseeable future, and as much as I want to run away again, I have nowhere else to go. Sure, I'm older now but no other bar is going to pay me what Ron does. Not to mention the heavily discounted apartment he allows me to live in. I also get the distinct impression you don't just walk away from Ron. I would be a liability, someone that knows too much to walk away free and clear.

"You can do this. Just focus on work. Just stay busy," I whisper to myself, trying to somehow reinforce the mask I wear, the mask that Declan doesn't even seem to notice.

A few deep breaths later, I feel calmer and raise my head to meet my gaze in the mirror. What I'm not expecting is to see Quinn behind me. I scream and jump around, so we're facing each other.

Something There In Between

"Did that fuck make you cry?" he says, taking a step toward me. He's so close to me now I can feel his breath fan across my face, his breath smells like beer and cigarettes. He's breathing heavily, and something about his eyes seems off. I can't quite place it, but he just doesn't look right. It also makes me nervous. I can't help but flash back to the look in Nate's eyes the night he raped me.

I lean back on the sink, bracing my arms behind me, trying to create some distance.

"Who?" I ask, confused and increasingly nervous about his proximity. Quinn's always had a thing for me, but he's never acted on it. Not one of the guys, except for Declan recently, has ever gotten this far into my personal space.

"Declan," Quinn spits out Declan's name like a profanity. His spit flies across my face, and I try not to cringe. Standing in front of him reminds me of being in a confrontation with an animal. *No sudden movements and maintain calm eye contact*, I remind myself.

"No, Declan didn't do anything. I just had some stuff on my mind." It's not really a lie, it's not really Declan's fault that I'm an emotional basket case.

Quinn just nods in response and reaches his hand up, running his fingers gently down my un-bruised cheek. He doesn't say another word after that, just turns and walks back out of the ladies' room.

I stand there for a minute or two, trying to figure out what just happened, before I shake my head and turn back around to the mirror. I refuse to add Quinn's strange behavior to the long list of shit I have on my mind. Fixing my hair in a sloppy bun, I head back to the bar.

Chapter 13

Declan

I feel bad after Bree all but runs to the bathroom. I feel especially bad when Greg looks at me from across the room, his eyes shooting to the bathroom door, then back at me before running his finger across his neck like he's slicing someone's throat. Jesus Christ.

Does Bree not realize that she has a family here? It's not conventional, by any means, but it's pretty obvious that's exactly what this group is. I notice Quinn following her to the bathroom, and I walk closer to that end of the bar to try to watch him. He pauses at the door, and gives me a chin lift, his mouth formed into an evil smirk, before he walks in. It takes everything in me to not leap over the bar top and follow him in. I try to listen, but I can't hear anything. I don't think Bree's in any danger but Quinn following her into the ladies' room makes no sense to me. He comes back out no more than 2 minutes later, and gives me a look that would make a lesser man cower. I stare right back into his eyes. I've already lived with the devil; there isn't much anyone else can do that will scare me. His eyes seem slightly glazed and his hands are clenching and unclenching as he finally breaks our staring contest to walk away.

Bree walks back behind the bar, and I feel like I need to do something to lighten the mood, so I look around. Then, I see Jake and, if it were possible, a light bulb would have lit up over my head. I mash my lips together trying to hide my devious grin and decide that the ass kicking I'm going to get is worth it.

"Hey, Lord Pussy Magnet!" I shout over the noise of people partying and music playing. Once Jake's horrendous high school nickname leaves my lips, it's like a scene from a movie where the music stops and everyone just stares at me. The majority of people are looking around, trying figure out who exactly 'Lord Pussy Magnet' is. My eyes scan the room until I find my brother's blonde faux hawk.

Jake's head snaps up, and he glowers as he walks toward me. "We had this conversation, Declan," he seethes almost under his breath. "That nickname is dead."

"Right, but as you're my only blood related family member left, it is my job, nay my privilege, to make sure that the truth is passed on throughout history, from generation to generation." My smile is all teeth.

Jake's face is getting redder by the second, and I am absolutely delighted. I turn to look at Bree, who walks closer to where we are standing. I'm leaning down on the bar, resting on my elbows, and Jake is standing directly in front of me on the other side of the bar. His face is pink, and his eyes are sending me all kinds of telepathic death threats, which I am completely ignoring. I steal another quick glance at Bree and that same left corner of her mouth starts to twitch and I know I've almost got her. It's now or never.

"Does anyone here know how you got that nickname?" I ask, putting on the most innocent face I can muster.

"That's my private business. I had crazy friends when I was younger," Jake snaps, looking around, before giving a nervous chuckle. As if I didn't know that would be the first excuse he pulled out of his ass.

"Bullshit. 1. You never had friends. 2. I distinctly remember you making that name up for yourself and feeling the need to tell everyone. I'm pretty sure you wrote it all over your backpack," I counter.

"You're gonna pay for this," Jake says. He's so cute when he thinks he's intimidating.

"When the illustrious Jake 'Lord Pussy Magnet' James here was in high school, he discovered the wonders of the female anatomy," I begin, as I notice a few more of the guys gathering around. Clearly, this is a story that hasn't been shared before. "My mother and I were in agreement that the girls must have been blind or drunk, but apparently Jake had somehow tricked some poor innocent girls into giving it up." I shoot Jake a condescending look, and he narrows his eyes at me.

"The first time 'Lord Pussy Magnet' made an appearance, it was on his backpack. It was written across one of the straps. I'm pretty sure our mother tore her rotator cuff trying to scrub it out. But the greatest and most noteworthy appearance of 'Lord Pussy Magnet' was when I caught Jake making out in the driveway of our house with yet another innocent victim." I'm flat out laughing now, the guys around Jake are cracking the fuck up, and even Jake is chuckling.

"So the car is a-rocking, as they say, and I hear the girl moan out Jake's name. Then, suddenly everything stops and I hear Jake say," I mimic his stern tone of voice from that night, but raise my voice a few notches. "No, baby, Jake isn't making you come. That's Lord Pussy Magnet," I finish, and turn to look at Bree.

All the breath leaves my body. She's smiling. She's not laughing, but she is full on smiling. She is magnificent.

A man could write songs about her smile. She looks at me, and shakes her head, before walking off to help a customer. I don't miss the fact that her shoulders are slightly shaking. Everyone around us is laughing their asses off. Even Jake has a huge grin on his face; his eyes are watering from trying so hard to keep his laugh in.

Everyone starts to walk away, laughing, and a few of the guys slap Jake on the back. He gives me a wry smile before glancing in Bree's direction. "That right there," Jake says his face now serious, "was worth it."

In this moment, I know I want to see her smile again. No, I need to see her smile again. I also know I will do anything in my power to make Bree not only smile more often, but to realize that her life is worth something. She is worth something.

S. Ferguson

Chapter 14

Bree

It's only been a few days since my first session with Ze, and I'm already back for more. The man is ruthless.

He is determined to push me past my limits. What scares me the most is, I don't think he means that just physically. He reminds me of Declan in a lot of ways. He's always watching me, and looking deeper into me than I would prefer. Right now, he has me in a plank, and the timer is set for two minutes. That doesn't seem so long, but have you ever done a plank for two minutes? Try it, then come back and tell me how easy it is. I'm a little nervous because Ze seems to have decided he wants to talk to me when I'm in a position like this, unable to move.

"You want to talk about it?" Ze asks nonchalantly. I grunt. Suddenly, the sweat breaking out all over my body has nothing to do with the workout.

"I know you don't want to talk, so I'll talk," he continues. "This kid, he was bad for you, yeah?"

I keep my head down. How does Ze even know about that? Ron has a big mouth. How do I even explain this? Alex wasn't bad. I was. I was the one who wasn't good enough for him, the reason he had to leave. We wouldn't have been in any of this mess if it weren't for me. The homelessness, the bar… that was all on me. Alex had run away with me to save me from Mother.

Ze doesn't seem shocked at all that I'm not answering him; he just keeps right on talking. "You think you're the only one who's had it, rough? My old man beat my ass every day until I left. He was a lot like Jake and Declan's dad. Granted, I think their old man was worse in the end. But your mother, she was a special kind of evil, wasn't she?"

This catches my attention for more than one reason. I've never told a soul, except for Alex, about Mother. Not one person. I've also never heard anyone but Declan on the night of… the night of the incident, talk about he and Jake's life before working for Ron. Before learning some of the story, Jake always seemed so *normal*. I couldn't have imagined him having had it too rough. But I do know that all of Ron's business isn't on the up and up, and the kinds of men who choose that lifestyle haven't always had the best life growing up.

"You know, I love my wife. I love her enough to take a bullet for her. If we were hungry, I would make sure she ate before I did. If we needed shelter, I would sell everything up to and including my own body to make sure she had somewhere safe to rest. Your boy… he didn't do any of this for you, did he?" Ze continues, following me as I finally finish the plank, and make my way to the punching bags. I can tell by the way he asks the question he already knows the answer.

"This boy, he fucked with your head and made you think this was your fault. The fact that he didn't love you enough to properly take care of you, if at all, the fact that he's the reason you were in that whole damn mess, he just let that all fall on your shoulders. He knew what your mother did to you, and he used that to his advantage. You were vulnerable, and he used that to try to finish you off. He was fucked up, but you and I both know this started before him. You were just ripe for the picking. That's what these assholes do."

"That boy saw how vulnerable you were, because he wasn't the first person to hurt you, was he? Not even close. No, he just wanted to deal the final blow."

I've had enough at this point. I keep hitting the bag, angry tears falling down my face, and my form goes to shit. My hands begin to hurt, but I don't stop, until I just can't take it anymore.

"It was my fault. You have no idea what you're talking about. It was on me!" I pound my chest angrily. It hurts, and part of me hopes it leaves a bruise, so the outside can match the inside. "I was the one that had to run away. You don't know what my life was like. You don't know anything about me."

I stand facing him, my chest heaving, tears continuing to fall, and I swipe the back of my hand across my face. The mixture of sweat and tears on my face causes my knuckles to sting, and I realize I've split two of them open on my right hand, where blood and sweat are mixing together, running down my fingers.

"But I do know you. I know more than you think. I'm actually thinking I may know more than you do. You think you're the first kid I've helped that had a shit life? Look around, baby girl. Everyone you know has had one. You think Ron was always happy and successful? You think Jake and the other boys didn't have a reason to start working for Ron? You think I had a good life? Why, because now, at fifty-five, I have my shit together? Everyone has a story, and their stories can help you, if you'll stop feeling sorry for yourself long enough to hear them. If you would listen to the truth, not this 'everything is my fault' shit you keep spoon-feeding yourself."

Ze's words are like a slap in the face. I want to be mad. I want to keep crying and… feeling sorry for myself. Realizing he's right, I only get angrier.

"Fuck you!" I shout, turning around and stomping to the women's locker room. Once inside, I sit down on the floor, just inside the door, and pull my knees up to my chest, wrapping my arms around them. Then, I lower my head. I want to cry, but my tears have mysteriously disappeared. I can't tell what makes me angrier: the fact that he's right, or the fact that he's taken away the only way I know how to deal with this. If I'm not feeling sorry for myself, then what am I supposed to be feeling? Am I supposed to be okay with Alex walking away from me? With my own mother hating me?

My life has been nothing but impossible choices. Always being forced to choose the lesser of two evils. My reality is far too much to bear. Accepting my life is impossible. Numbing things the best I can, and being cocooned in my sorrow, are the only ways I can keep my head above water. I know this because I've done it for years now. I don't know how to be any other way. There is safety in the familiar. My sorrow keeps my pain away. But that's a lie. I spend every single day in pain, my heart mourning for what it's lost, what it never even had in some cases.

What if everything you've been telling yourself is a lie, just like that one?

The thought comes unbidden, and I immediately push it aside. I can't fathom a world where anyone but me is to blame. My mother abused me because I was *me*. Alex left me because I was *me*. This is my truth.

I hear a light tapping on the door, followed by Ze's voice coming through the door. "This is the first step, baby girl. Tomorrow, we start really training."

I lift my head, and it hits the wall behind me with a thud. I shake my head and give an angry sigh. He's right because I don't know if I can go back to my pity party after this.

He's right that I'm going to come back tomorrow. He's right because somehow, even in the midst of my anger, I know things will never be the same after this.

Chapter 15

Declan

Something is wrong. Something is off with Bree. I didn't think she could get any more quiet, but apparently she can. Ron seemed unconcerned when I mentioned it in passing as I first got to work. Now, I can see he is watching her a little more intently than normal. I try to stop myself from asking her what's wrong.

I made it longer than I thought I would be able to, but as the bar is winding down and I'm on hour five of another Bree-is-acting-stranger-than-normal shift, I notice she has bruises and some split knuckles. That does it for me.

The idea that someone is hurting her causes a rage I've only ever felt once before in my life to flow through my entire body. I clench my fists and decide now is the moment I confront her. Is there another asshole bothering her now? Did her douchebag ex make an appearance? I will fucking end whoever did this to her. I know without asking that Jake would have my back on that move. I'd be willing to bet money Ron would as well. It takes every ounce of strength I have, but I wait until the night is a little closer to being over before snatching her arm and pulling her through the doorway into the dark kitchen. I spin her around to the wall beside the doorway, leaning down so we're face to face, eye to eye.

"You're gonna tell me what the fuck is going on, and you're gonna tell me right the fuck now. Is someone hurting you? Why are your knuckles all bruised? You been fighting?" I fire off everything at once, realizing I sound like a nagging girlfriend, but I need to know she's okay. I NEED to get this off my chest.

Bree sighs deeply, her warm breath fanning across my neck, making me aware of our proximity. I have her pinned to the wall, my left hand is still gripping her shoulder, and my right hand is on the wall above her head. I'm being a bastard, and using my size to cage her in. I watch her closely for signs of fear, but she almost looks bored, and mostly just annoyed. I know she can still refuse to answer, but I'll be damned if she gets away from me until I have my say.

She raises her eyes to give me an angry glare and I feel my dick twitch. Seeing fire in her eyes as opposed to the sadness they always carry makes her ten times hotter. Fuck, I'm an asshole. Something is seriously wrong with her, and I'm standing here getting turned on.

"I've just had a lot on my mind. I've been...training. You know exercising and punching a bag. That's why my knuckles are bruised." She raises an eyebrow at me, daring me to question her more. I smirk down at her... she has no idea who she's messing with.

"You need to wear gloves then. You're going to ruin your beautiful hands. You're not actually sparring are you?" I ask, my voice deeper than I intended. I've never been this close to her before, and my dick is currently trying to punch its way out of my zipper to reach her.

She glances down, and I have a moment of horror when I realize there is no way she's going to miss my erection. I'm a healthy boy, and my jeans were already on the tight side. Her breath hitches, and she jerks her eyes back up to meet mine.

When I see the heat in her eyes, I swear I almost come in my pants like a teenager. Bree is fucking turned on by me. I can work with this. Letting go of her shoulder, I put my hand on the wall, completely closing her in, and lower my head towards hers.

"I don't fool around with Ron's guys," she says softly, making no move to avoid my quickly approaching lips.

"Good thing I'm not one then," I say, my mouth forming a smirk. I'm now so close to her lips I can feel their warmth on my own.

"YO BREE, where ya at?" I hear Jake yell from outside the door. His voice is like a splash of cold water, causing me to jerk back, and the moment is gone.

"My brother is an asshole," I grumble, lowering my hands to adjust my erection, and backing further away from her.

"Your brother just stopped me from making a stupid mistake," she says, before walking out of the door.

I hear her call out to Jake as the door closes behind her. I stay back a few minutes, willing the jerk in my pants to calm down. I can't remember the last time I was this turned on. Shit, Candice was swallowing my cock and it wasn't this hard.

Once I feel like I won't traumatize anyone, I make my way back to the bar. Jake is talking to Bree, wildly gesturing with his hands.

Before I can get to them, I hear a screech and I grunt as something small and hard slams into my body. I actually stumble back from the impact.

"Oh my God, baby, where have you been? I've been looking everywhere for you!" Candice whines into my chest.

I look around, once again thinking this has to be some sort of prank, but considering Candice has not stopped her incessant calls and texts, despite me never answering or acknowledging them, added to the fact she's now shown up at the bar, it's becomes clear to me that she is really is bat shit crazy.

As gently, yet forcefully, as I can, I extract myself from her death grip and look down into her crazy ass eyes.

"Look, this whole thing has really gotten carried away. I'm sorry if I did anything to lead you on, but I'm not looking for a relationship or anything really. I had a great time that night, but that's what we need to leave it at. You understand, right?" I say, and immediately regret it.

Candice's brown eyes turn dark with fury, and I see her chest begin to move quickly as she takes several gulps of air before unleashing on me.

I tune out her screaming, catching the occasional "asshole" as I look around frantically for someone to help me.

Most of the guys are ignoring the situation; it's not the first time some crazy bitch has shown up screaming at a guy here. Definitely won't be the last. Jake is doubled over in laughter, and Bree is standing there staring at me with her eyes wide. *Help*, I mouth at her. She makes an annoyed face before marching towards us.

"….and you just threw it away!" Candice slaps my arm, bringing my attention back to her. I've never hit a woman, and I definitely never will, but I find myself wondering how much of an asshole it would make me if choked her. Maybe I could just push her out of the bar?

"Look, he's moved on. You're embarrassing yourself. Just stop." Bree's voice is firm as she comes to stand next to me. I don't know if her intent was to imply she is Candice's replacement or not, but I'm rolling with it. I grab Bree and bring her to my side, tucking her under my arm, and kissing the top of her head. She brings her foot down hard on top of mine, but I ignore it. It feels like she broke my toe. So worth it.

"WHAAAAAAAT???????" Candice screeches, and, I swear to God, nails on a chalkboard are a more pleasant sound.

I don't have to look down at Bree to know she's giving me a death glare. "She's right. I was just trying to let you down gently. Please, have some self-respect and let's just walk away." I give Bree a squeeze to help make my point.

I should have seen it coming. As a man in general, especially as someone who's dealt with more than one angry woman in my lifetime, I really should have known what Candice's next move would be. Her eye twitches, and then pain radiates in my lower stomach. That crazy bitch just kneed me in the balls. I fall to my knees, cupping my boys, tears welling in my eyes. I hear some scuffling and more screeching from Candice, but I'm in far too much agony to bother looking. Kill me. Kill me now.

Chapter 16

Bree

I'm not someone who usually delights in the pain of others but when Declan hits the floor I would have laughed my ass off except I found myself with an armful of pissed off blonde. Candice launched her body at mine with more strength than I would have guessed she had. I stepped back on my right foot, putting my body at an angle, and managing to keep my balance. Suddenly, I am very thankful for all my lessons with Ze.

Apparently, he was on a mission to make sure what happened…well, he wanted to make sure I could prevent that from happening ever again. Her right arm shoots out to hit me, and I see my opportunity. I quickly grab her wrist with my right hand, rotating her arm towards her body at the same time keeping her arm straight, before I slam my left forearm down on her elbow.

She screeches as her body is forced to bend in half, and she lowers down to one knee, trying to relieve the pressure on her arm. The next move Ze taught me in this scenario is a knee to the face and, man, is it tempting.

I keep her arm locked in the uncomfortable position, and my voice steady and even. She obviously knows if I put more pressure on her arm, it's going to break. A broken arm is bad, but an arm broken at the elbow? She would be lucky if she ever got to use it again.

"Touch me again, and this arm will belong to me." I'm almost proud of the menace I can hear in my voice. She glares at me but nods. Before I can release her, Ron steps up. He gives her a look I've never seen on his face before, somewhere between rage and disgust.

"You ever come back here again, you'll wish for death before I'm done with you," he pauses making sure Candice is listening. "Bree is one of us. Declan is one of us, and you just fucking attacked them…in my motherfucking house. That means you may as well have attacked me. If you were a man, I would have already put a bullet in your skull. This is your one free pass."

Candice visibly swallows, nodding her head more frantically. I quickly release her and back up, keeping my feet shoulder width apart, and my arms slightly bent, ready for another attack.

I really can't wait to tell Ze about this. He should be damn proud of me, after he makes me run laps for using violence when it wasn't completely necessary. But she did attack me; I can plead my case.

"This isn't over, you bitch," Candice hisses as she rubs her right arm and hobbles off.

"That was hot as shit. If I could get hard right now, I totally would," Declan wheezes from the ground.

"Get up. You're embarrassing yourself," I say before walking back to the bar. Once I'm there, I realize I'm smiling, widely. For once, I don't feel guilty. Maybe it's okay to be a little happy sometimes?

Once the drama calms down, the guys all go back to their pool games and gossip. Yes, these guys gossip. Being so quiet has its advantages. I know way more about these guys than I should, but I'm not one to talk about them. Half the time it's just gross stuff about their sex lives anyway.

Declan emerges from Ron's office after hiding for about 10 minutes. I'm pretty sure he was icing his balls.

"So, we gonna talk about how you're a ninja?" he teases me as he sits down delicately on a stool across from me.

"I may have learned a little bit about defending myself." I want to tell him about Ze, but I just can't. I don't know why it's so hard for me to just have a conversation. He's not asking me about anything abnormal. I just can't open up; these walls have been in place so long even I can't bring them down.

"That was more than a little bit. That's real training. Guess you were telling the truth about your knuckles." He nods his head towards my hands. An unbidden image of us in the kitchen flashes through my brain, only this time Jake doesn't ruin the moment and

Declan's mouth is on mine. My breath hitches, and I feel my body clench in response.

"Tell me what you're thinking," Declan says, his voice having a rasp to it that wasn't there a minute ago. I bite my bottom lip and meet his gaze. I can feel the heat in my cheeks.

"Just thinking about training," I lie. I don't think Declan buys it, judging by the smirk he's giving me, but he doesn't say anything.

"You working out, or just learning to kick ass?" He reaches over the counter and grabs a handful of orange slices.

"You bastard! I had to cut all of those. You wanna snack on them, go cut some yourself!" I growl at him and swat at him with my cleaning rag.

"It's almost closing time and look around. It's only Ron's guys here now, and they aren't the kind who gets orange slices on their drinks. Except maybe Jake. Does he still drink that fruity shit?" He scrunches up his face in thought, and it might be the most adorable thing I've ever seen.

"No, Jake's a straight bourbon and beer these days. Might wanna keep that little tidbit to yourself, you know, man card and all," I say, making myself smile. This is good. It's good to talk and smile and be friends. Right?

Declan throws his head back, and barks out a laugh, before speaking again. "What's funny is you think he had a man card at all."

I give a little snort, and start to walk away, but Declan reaches out and grabs my arm.

"I like this side of you. I've never had this long of a conversation with you, or seen you smile so much in one night, or you know, smile *ever*. I like you even when you're walking around like Wednesday Adams, but I *really* like you when you're being Bree." His voice is almost a whisper, but I hear it all the way to my soul. I feel a flicker of warmth in my chest.

"You don't know Bree," I whisper back, telling me, more than him. He doesn't know what a damaged waste of time I am.

"I don't know all of Bree, yet," he corrects me, "but I will." With that, he lets go of my arm and I make a quick escape. I distract myself with being busy with whatever random task I can find, but I never stop thinking about his words for the rest of the night.

S. Ferguson

Chapter 17

Declan

I walked home that night with a limp in my step and a giant smile on my face. Progress. I've made progress with Bree.

I feel like she's slowly starting to open up. I find myself wandering to the park and standing guard over her as she sits on her bench tonight, and I have full intentions of doing this every night. It might just be me, but I feel like she's spending less and less time out there each night. Last night, I leaned against her building and watched her listen to her music, staring off into space. Only this time, I caught her head moving with the music and she only sits for about half the time she did on the first night I watched her. Progress.

The next afternoon, after my run, I decide I've really been putting off grocery shopping. I hate it. I know how to cook, but cooking for one is pretty fucking stupid. I just don't think I can eat another meal that's take out. Then, an idea pops into my head. Scrolling through my phone, I find Bree's number. She probably doesn't know I have it, but Ron gave it to me with instructions to use it for emergencies only.

Desperately needing groceries is an emergency, right? I tap my thumbs across the screen, wishing for the hundredth time that the screen was bigger or my thumbs were smaller.

Yo. Let's get groceries. The state of my kitchen is horrifying.

I watch my phone like a fucking teenage girl for the next five minutes.

Who is this?

I probably should have said who I was to begin with. Damn it. Oh well too late now. I decide to have some fun.

It's the man of your dreams B Girl. I want to take you away to a magical land called Whole Foods. They have everything you've ever dreamed of, for twice the price of any other place.

I stare at my phone, grinning like an idiot, and waiting for her response.

Yeah, that's really not helpful. I don't know how you got my number but lose it.

Okay, does she not have a sense of humor? Wait, what time is it? I look at the clock and cringe. Yeah, it's 3 o'clock in the afternoon; she just finished training. She won't tell me much about it, but I know she goes every day at one in the afternoon. She's probably worn out and in a foul mood. If I were a better man, I would feel bad, but seeing Bree is far too important to me.

Obviously you haven't recovered from your workout yet so I'll stop teasing ya. It's Dec. I'll be at yours in 20 with coffee. How do you take it?

This time, she only takes one minute to answer.

Black like my soul.

I grin, and shove my phone in my pocket, before grabbing my keys and heading out the door. The line at Starbucks is astronomical, so it ends up being more like thirty minutes before I walk around the corner to Bree's building. She's standing outside with her arms crossed over her chest, trying to keep warm. I take a minute to check her out, slowing my pace. She's wearing one of those cute beanie hats that are way too big, a military-style jacket, and black skinny jeans with those ankle boot things girls like on her feet. Her eyes are lined in black eyeliner, and her lips have a slight sheen to them. I'm guessing lip-gloss or whatever the fuck it is chicks use that make their lips shiny. That shit usually tastes good, too. Immediately, my mind wonders what flavor Bree's lips are, and my dick gives a little twitch. I quickly change my focus.

"Sorry, I took a bit longer than planned. The line was a bitch." I hold her coffee out to her. She takes it with both hands, and uses it like a tiny heater.

"S'okay, coffee makes everything better." She takes a careful sip of the hot liquid and closes her eyes, humming in appreciation. Interesting. So coffee is definitely high on Bree's list of priorities. Maybe she really is my fucking soulmate.

"Anyhoo, I dragged you out this fine day because I am in dire need of real food. As much as I love being on a first name basis with every delivery driver in town, I need real sustenance," I say, putting my hand on her lower back and gently nudging her in the direction we need to walk.

"Right, but how does this concern me?" she asks, between sips of her coffee. It's gotta be somewhere between the fires of hell and lava in temperature, but she doesn't seem to care.

"I need help and you need to get out and live a little, so we're gonna start with you helping me grocery shop. Girls know all about that shit anyway. If I go alone, I'll just end up with beer. Baby steps, ya know?" I say, leaning toward her and nudging her arm with mine. She rolls her eyes, and I'm pretty sure she's smirking, but it's hard to tell with the coffee cup that is glued to her face.

We walk a good block before she breaks the silence. "I'm not really good at this. I mean, with people. I don't really know what to do with you," she says, then bites on her bottom lip and turns her face away, but not before I see the pink tinge in her cheeks.

I stop and grab her shoulder, turning her to face me. She looks so tiny under that big beanie, her hair still damp and hanging over her shoulders. "What do you mean?"

"I mean, most guys I'm around, I know what they want. They want to hook up or they want me to serve them a drink. That's what I do. I only know how to do that," she says, raising her eyes to look at me. I can see some defiance in them, like she's expecting me to judge her.

"Well, if the guys you've been around only want those two things from you, then they're assholes. I, B Girl, am not an asshole." I scoff like its common knowledge.

"Okay, maybe I should put it this way, what do you want from me…because I'm not hooking up with you. I never hook up with Ron's guys. And there isn't a bar here." Bree looks right in my eyes as she says this, and I know this is a pivotal moment. If I answer this wrong, she's gonna shut right back up, and I'm going to lose all the progress we're making.

"I just wanna go grocery shopping. If you're super helpful, I may throw in lunch for you. How's that sound?" I ask, holding my elbow out for her to grab.

I grin, as Bree reluctantly loops her arm through mine. "Groceries it is, then." We walk the rest of the way to the store in a comfortable silence.

Once I've grabbed a cart, I steer her towards the produce section. "What exactly are you looking for?" She looks kind of lost, turning around, and looking at all the fresh fruit and vegetables.

"You don't cook, do you?" I ask, grabbing some bananas.

"Not really. My… I never learned how," she says, sadness flashes across her face.

"I'm not the best cook either, but my mom taught me a little bit. My challenge is more cooking for just one." I throw some apples in a bag, before weighing them and putting them in the cart.

"You eat alone often?" she asks quietly.

"You offering to come eat with me?" I say with a grin. I can't help but wonder if that's her way of finding out if I'm single or a manwhore... wouldn't blame her after the Crazy Candice fiasco.

"Maybe. If you can guarantee you won't give me food poisoning," she teases, running her hands over some tomatoes.

"Grab me some of those, like six, I wanna make salsa," I say, grabbing some onion, and looking back at her. I immediately burst into laughter as I watch her meticulously pick up each tomato, smell it, and then either put it in one of the produce bags or back on the display.

"What in the actual fuck are you doing?" I wheeze.

"You have to smell them. If they don't smell right, they won't be good." She gives me a 'Duh' look.

"I've never in my life smelled a tomato. How can you even smell anything? The skin is still on it." I return her 'Duh' look.

"I'm kind of a connoisseur of tomatoes. Just trust me on this." She makes a point of turning away from me, as dramatically as possible, and continues smelling the tomatoes before she either puts them back or into the bag.

We spend the rest of our shopping expedition, continuing the light banter, and she smiles more than I think she ever has in an entire day since I've known her. Maybe in her entire life. When the cashier gives me my total, she makes big eyes at me and I laugh.

"I told you they would charge me twice as much as anywhere else, but it's worth it." I grab the bags and look over my shoulder as she follows me out of the store. "Get an Uber, will you? I'm not carrying all this shit back to my apartment." I dig my phone out of my pocket and motion for her to grab it.

She takes my phone and orders the Uber while we sit on a bench outside, waiting. I feel like I should Google benches and symbolism; there always seems to be one involved with Bree.

After a quick Uber ride, we're outside my building and Bree's holding the bulk of the bags while I use one hand to dig my keys out.

"I told you that you should have gotten those out while we were still in the car." She really is a smartass. Soul. Mate.

"Yeah yeah yeah. Come on." I hold the door open, as she slips under my arm and starts up the stairs.

"First door on the right," I guide her as we reach the second floor, then I mentally shake my head. She knows where the apartment is; I doubt she's forgotten that night.

Opening my apartment door, I head straight for the kitchen and drop my load on the counter. This is the worst part of grocery shopping in my opinion, having to put all the shit away, especially in my tiny-ass kitchen. We make quick work of it, and I realize we really do work well together. At the bar, in my small kitchen, we just flow. We never get in each other's way.

After my mountain of food has been put away, I decide it's time to make good on my offer to take her to lunch. "Where do you wanna go eat?" I ask her, closing the door to my now-organized pantry with triumphant glee. Bree totally reorganized it while getting irritated trying to find space for all my new items. Total win for me.

"You're really going to get takeout after buying all these groceries in order to avoid take out?" Bree's face is incredulous.

"You bet I am." I don't miss a beat.

"You owe me Chipotle then for that hot mess," she says, exasperatedly.

"Done!" I raise my hand for a high five. She rolls her eyes at me, and makes her way to the apartment door.

After grabbing Chipotle to go, lucky me has one located on the same block as my apartment, we find ourselves back in my living room.

"So, how about I make some salsa, and it can chill in the fridge while we watch a movie until we're ready for more food?" I suggest, realizing too late how cheesy that suggestion sounds.

"Netflix and chill?" she asks, giving me a mocking look.

Instead of answering, I waggle my eyebrows lecherously at her and start pulling the ingredients for salsa.

Once the salsa is made and chilling in the fridge, I give Bree first pick of my DVD collection, and make myself comfortable on my love seat. The apartment is too small for a full-size couch. It always annoyed me because I could never just lie down and watch a movie, but suddenly it's pretty damn convenient. I sprawl out, taking up as much room as possible, so she'll be forced to sit close.

"You have got to be fucking kidding me," Bree says, looking at the loveseat and then me.

"What? You know how fucking expensive the cost of living is here, and a full-size couch wouldn't fit. We'll be fine. I showered this morning and everything." I pat the cushion next to me.

She sits down, and then toes off her ankle boots, before bringing her knees up under her chin and wrapping her arms around her shins. I spread out with one arm behind her, and my legs spread wide so my thigh is brushing against hers.

The movie starts and I am momentarily stunned. She picked *Equilibrium*. Not many people know about this cult-classic, so I decide to see if it was a random choice or if she knows how magnificent it truly is.

"You know this isn't a romance, right?" I say, casually grabbing a lock of her hair, and twirling it in my fingers. It's way softer than I imagined. Not that I've imagined it. Not too often anyway.

"Yes, I know it's not a romance. His wife is killed, and then he watches the other chick die, too," Bree says, shooting me a stern look and pulling her hair from in between my fingers. So, she *does* know the movie. Interesting.

"I totally think this movie was a big inspiration for the Matrix. The whole fighting style and outfits. Total rip off." I catch another strand of her hair and begin twirling it again.

She sighs and takes her beanie off, moving her hair further away from me. She runs her fingers through all of her hair, straightening it from having had the beanie on it.

The movement causes her scent to drift over. She smells like vanilla. I inhale deeply, and try to keep my eyes from rolling back in my head.

"Do you wanna watch the movie, or do you want to keep talking?" she cocks an eyebrow at me.

"Movie's good," I say, grabbing her shoulder and bringing her back to rest against the back of the loveseat. I may also start twirling her hair again.

About halfway through the movie, I realize that I can't ignore how close to me she is. Her vanilla sent seems to be taking over my apartment, but in the best way. She seems to be engrossed in the movie, but I honestly couldn't tell you anything that is happening. Deciding I can't take it anymore, I reach over and grab her legs, stretching them out, so they are lying across my lap.

"What are you doing?" she asks, but I can tell it's half-hearted.

"Just making sure you're comfortable. This couch isn't big, but you're small enough to make it work. One of us should at least be comfortable." I keep my hand on her leg. She's so small that my hand almost covers her entire thigh.

"This isn't a couch and this isn't a date," she says, but she turns her attention back to the television, leaving her legs where they are.

I consider this a win, and start absentmindedly running my hand up and down her thigh, getting closer and closer to the V between them. I can tell she's not immune because she begins to shift, rubbing her legs together slightly. She's not the only one getting worked up. I'm harder than I've ever been in my life. There is no way she can't feel it under her legs.

"Declan." My name is a whisper leaving her mouth.

I turn to look at her, and the heat in her eyes takes my breath away. She wants this as much as I do. She opens her mouth to say something, but I beat her to it.

"Shhhh. Don't think so hard. Just go with it," I say, and my voice is rough. I have no hope she hasn't noticed how turned on I sound.

She stays quiet, but leans her head back against the arm of the loveseat, and closes her eyes. I take this as my chance, and use my hands to spread her thighs slightly. I watch her face closely, but she doesn't open her eyes. I gently cup her sex over her jeans. Her breath hitches, and her eyes open, staring straight into mine.

"Dec…" her voice trails off. Hearing my name leave her lips, and how turned on she is, makes me lose my goddamn mind. Before she can change her mind, I gently lift her up, she's so light, and I place her in my lap. There's no way in hell she can't feel how excited I am now.

"I don't think this is a good idea." Her eyes don't meet mine.

"If you tell me to stop, I'll stop, B girl," I whisper, cupping the side of her face in my hand. I turn her so she's facing me.

"I don't know if I can," she whispers back. She bites her bottom lip, and I use my thumb to pull it out. Very slowly, watching her eyes for any sign of protest, I lean forward and run my tongue across the abused lip.

I hear her swift intake of breath, and it's like a starting gun at the races. My hand moves from the side of her face to the back of her head, and grabbing a fistful of her hair, I tilt her head sideways and press my mouth to hers.

Her hands fly up and she grabs my shoulders.

I take a moment to make sure she's grabbing and not pushing. Satisfied she isn't fighting this, I sweep my tongue in to taste her. She's the sweetest thing I've ever tasted.

Her tongue tangles with mine, and I groan from the sensation. I feel like I've sprung some sort of leak in my pants. I don't think I've ever been this turned on.

Bree moans into my mouth, and twists her body around, placing a thigh on either side of my legs, and straddling me. My free hand immediately flies to her ass. It feels even better than I could have ever imagined. I pull her toward me, pressing her warm heat right where I want her.

She gasps into my mouth, and begins to gently grind against me. We make out like this for what feels like hours, but is probably only a few minutes.

I feel the familiar tingle at the base of my spine, and realize I'm about to come from dry humping. I don't think that's happened since I was a teenager.

"B Girl... Babe, we gotta slow down," I say, hating myself the minute the words leave my mouth.

She immediately pulls her mouth off mine and tries to climb off me. I grab her hips, holding her place. "I didn't say stop.

I said slow down. We keep this up, and I'm gonna have a mess in my pants." I'm not too proud to admit how much she turns me on.

"Oh, yeah, right," Bree snorts and rolls her eyes.

"Exactly, right," I say, looking in her eyes. "Do you have any idea how fucking sexy you are? Touching you, tasting you… it's more than a guy can take," I tell her honestly. I know she needs to hear this.

"Um, if you say so," she says, still not meeting my eyes.

"I need to know how far you want to go. Can I eat your pretty pussy?" I ask, throwing in a cheesy grin.

"You've never seen it. How do you know it's pretty?" Good. Smartass Bree is back.

"A girl like you wouldn't be anything but gorgeous on every inch of her body. Please let me taste you?" I probably sound like I'm begging, but I couldn't give a fuck. Bree deserves to hear it, to know that she's worth begging for.

"I don't do blow jobs," she states like that settles it.

"Did I ask you to blow me?" I ask her, lifting her chin so she's looking at me.

"I don't understand." That bottom lip is between her teeth again.

"I want to taste you. I want to eat that pretty little pussy, and make you come in my mouth. That's what I'm asking you. Can I do that please? I wanna hear you scream in pleasure. I want to know that I gave that to you," I tell her, my eyes never leaving hers. She gives me a slight nod of her head. I'll take it. I stand with her still wrapped around me, her eyes growing large.

"I love how tiny you are. I can just pick you up and move. I don't have to lose your warmth." I grin at her and turn, before sitting her back down on the loveseat in front of me.

I drop to me knees in front of her. I feel like a starving man staring at a feast laid out just for him.

"Look at me," I command, slowly raising my hands to the button of her jeans. She blushes, but meets my gaze. I make quick work of unzipping them, and ask her to lift her hips, so I can pull them down. I give them a hard tug and she squeals. The jeans don't move, not even a centimeter.

"Um?" I scratch my head.

"Sorry, they're kind of tight. Hang on." She turns, so she's lying down, and starts doing some sort of impression of a person having an exorcism while she yanks them down. They're so tight her feet can barely even slip out.

"I'm not saying I don't love the way you look in tight jeans, because I do, but seriously that can't be healthy," I say, tossing them over my shoulder. She's wearing black boy shorts.

Soulmate. Boy shorts are my kryptonite. There's something so sexy and playful about them. I'll take them over a thong any day.

"Are we gonna talk about my health, or are you gonna get back to the task at hand?" she asks, cocking an eyebrow.

Seeing she's returned to the sitting position, I decide to let my actions speak for themselves and bury my face in her boy shorts. I can smell her through them, all woman, clean with a little musk. Bree. She smells like Bree. And she smells like mine.

I kiss her through the thin material, kissing her just like I did with her mouth a few minutes earlier. She puts her legs on my shoulders and moans. I slide a finger in the side of her panties and my finger finds its way between her folds. She's so fucking wet. My dick gives a sympathetic spurt of pre-cum, and I moan long and low.

Regretfully pulling my finger from her, I grab the waistband of the boy shorts and pull them down her legs. I pull her towards me, so she's perched on the edge of the cushion, before spreading her thighs and looking at her for the first time. She's bare, all pretty and pink and glistening for me. I think my eyes roll back in my head.

I go back to kissing her with gusto, my tongue tracing her lips to the top and finding her clit. I give her a few licks there, and she grabs my hair. I smile against her and open my eyes. Her face is clenched in concentration, and she looks fucking adorable. I pull my mouth back, ignoring her small grunt of protest.

"So, how do you like it? You all clit, want some fingers? How do we feel about ass play?" I ask, mainly just wanting to see her reaction.

"Are you fucking serious?" she asks, opening up her eyes. She looks pissed.

Before I can answer, she reaches up and grabs the back of my head, nearly slamming my face into her core. I laugh against her, and start licking everywhere I can. I devour her. She's getting wetter and wetter. The muscles in her thighs are tensing, and her legs are shaking. I can see the tendons straining. I can hear her moaning and panting, but it takes me a minute to realize she's saying something.

"Please, please please," she's chanting over and over again.

She doesn't have to ask me twice. I thrust two fingers into her quickly, reaching until I find that spongy spot, and make a come hither motion with my fingers. Her back arches off the couch and she screams. As in, for real screams. I would have tried to cover her mouth with my free hand, but I was too busy drowning.

It would seem that Bree is what the porn industry lovingly calls a squirter. I pull my mouth away, but continue moving my fingers in and out of her, working her through it.

I don't think I've ever seen someone come so hard. I want to pound my fists on my chest like the Neanderthal that I am.

She finally relaxes back against the pillows and opens her eyes. She looks sleepy and satisfied. She catches her breath, and then a look of horror crosses her face.

"Oh my God, did I pee on you? I… that's never happened to me before…" She looks bright red, and starts frantically searching for her underwear.

I push her back and kiss her thoroughly, knowing she can taste herself on my lips, and being even more turned on by it.

My cock gives a twitch, reminding me that he still needs attention, but I tell him to knock it off. This was for Bree. We're not going to have sex today. I want to make her mine more than anything, and today started that, but she needs to know I'm not just after one thing from her. I'm not every other asshole she's been with before.

"Haven't done what before, had an orgasm from oral or squirted?" I ask, palming my dick through my jeans, and looking at her still exposed pussy.

"First of all, please don't ever say the word squirt or any variation of it again, that's just gross. And I've never…" Her voice trails off and she mumbles the last part of the sentence.

"You've never what?" I ask, deciding fuck it, I'm totally about to jerk off in front of her or my nuts will fall off.

"Never had an orgasm. Ever. Never tried oral sex before, but it hasn't worked well with the um… traditional way either."

She looks really nervous, like I'm going to think something is wrong with her.

"First of all, that makes me proud as fuck that I got to be the first guy to taste you. Second, that makes me proud as fuck, again, that I get to be responsible for your first orgasm ever. Speaking of orgasms, I need to have one really quick, so just stay right there." I move quickly opening my pants and letting my dick spring free. I spit in my hand unceremoniously and start jerking myself off.

This isn't going to take long. I should be embarrassed by how close I am to coming already, but I'm too far gone to give a fuck.

I look up from between Bree's legs to see her face. She's turned on again, I can tell. Her mouth is slightly parted, and her eyes are glazed over again. She shocks the shit out of my by raising her legs back to the edge of the cushion and spreading herself wide.

I get a perfect view of her glistening pussy. My balls pull tight.

"Do it, Dec. Come for me," she says, trailing a finger down, and slowly pushing it into her entrance. That does it. I come so hard my vision goes white, and I have to catch myself with my left hand on the floor, so I don't fall on my face.

Once I catch my breath, I look up at Bree. She's put her boy shorts back on, and she's laughing really hard.

"What?" I ask, looking around trying to figure out what's so funny. When I turn my head, something moves in the corner of my vision, and I reach my hand up. It's cum. I came on my own fucking head.

How is that even possible?

"I…um…I don't think I've ever seen someone have that straight of aim before. Also, great distance. I always thought the chest was a good cum-shot. You're an overachiever," she says before snorting and laughing all over again.

"Whatever," I mumble, pulling my shirt over my head, and using it wipe the semen off my head. I'm totally laughing about this later when I'm alone.

"You're…you're in really good shape. Really good," Bree says, bringing my attention back to her again. She's biting that fucking bottom lip again, and openly perusing my body.

"I'm glad you like it. You can enjoy it any time you like," I say, dropping my shirt and crawling towards her.

My cock is making a valiant attempt to rise again so soon after an orgasm, and I can tell my little performance reignited Bree.

I give a playful growl before tackling her to the back of the couch and kissing her like my life depends on it. She wraps her legs and arms around me, trying to lay me on top of her, but there isn't room on this tiny ass loveseat.

"Hang on, spider monkey," I whisper, standing with her clinging to me. I only stumble twice taking us to my bedroom. I hate my tiny ass bed but it's still better than the loveseat. I lie down with her on top of me. She rests her elbows on either side of my head, and looks in my eyes. For once, I didn't have to ask her to look at me. Progress.

"Thank you." She gives me a sincere look.

"You don't ever have to thank me for giving you orgasms. It's my pleasure. Nay, it's my privilege. I pledge you my life and limb," I grind up into her meaningfully, "To give you as many orgasms as your heart desires, whenever your heart desires them." My fake British accent is terrible, but she's laughing too hard to notice.

She's laughing. Hearing her laugh, hearing her moans, tasting her, feeling her, I know there is no going back from this for me. I don't know how to. She's going to be everything to me, soon. I can feel it.

Bree leans down, nuzzling into my neck, and I wrap my arms around her tightly.

"I forgot how it feels to be held. It's been so long," she whispers, so quietly I almost don't hear her. I ignore the feeling of her tears in my neck, allowing her this moment.

"You deserve to be held, Bree. You deserve orgasms, too. Lots and lots of orgasms," I growl, flipping her over and diving onto her giggling body. Apparently, this is the wrong thing to do because Bree's entire body stiffens and she pulls away from me. I give a deep sigh, watching her stand up and make her way back to the living room where her clothes are.

I can feel all our progress start to slip away the minute Bree puts her pants back on. Her walls flew back up so fast, I wouldn't have believed they'd come down at all if I hadn't just witnessed it myself just a few minutes ago.

I knew she wouldn't want to watch another movie, but I had to try. "I'm sure the salsa's ready now. We can have a snack and watch another movie?" I knew her answer before I finished asking the question.

"Look, Declan, this really wasn't a smart idea. You just got off the crazy train and I'm…I'm really not capable of more than what we just did," she says with a small, sad sigh. I can see the honesty in Bree's eyes. She really believes what she's saying.

"What we just did was fuckin' perfect, B Girl. I'm not asking for anything…yet. You're not ready, but when you are, and believe me you will be, I'll be right here. For now, let's just live in the moment. Can we do that?" This time, it's my eyes showing honesty.

"I don't know…I just…I need to go home." Just like that, she makes quick work of getting her shoes on and is out the door a few moments later.

It takes a good five minutes before I realize I'm just standing in the middle of my apartment, staring at my door like an asshole. Clearly, getting Bree to open up is going to be more of a challenge than I thought. Good thing I'm up for it.

S. Ferguson

Chapter 18

Bree

I don't even contemplate stopping at my bench tonight. I make short work of the walk home, and head straight to the shower once I make it inside. I need to clear my head. I'm not even sure what just happened.

Once I'm under the warm water, with the steam filling the air around me, I close my eyes and rethink the day's events. Dec texting was so unexpected, but I am so happy he did.

I can't remember the last time I felt those butterflies in my stomach. I also can't remember the last time I heard from a guy, and it wasn't just because he wanted a booty call. But that's exactly what it turned into, wasn't it?

Despite the logic to that thought process, something in me rejects it. Declan has never hid his attraction, and he didn't use me. I can admit I would have gone along with almost anything he wanted today, and all he did was please me. He even jerked himself off. This is so confusing.

I turn around, so the water cascades down my face and then make quick work of washing my hair.

Why didn't he let me touch him? Why does he act like he doesn't want anything from me? Everyone wants something. Why wasn't he weirded out by my questions? Did I totally blow it by running out of there like my ass was on fire?

Turns out, taking a shower to try and clear my head is a horrible idea because I am even more confused when I finish.

Wrapping myself up in a fluffy robe, I brush the tangles from my hair, and put in leave-in conditioner. My habit of constantly using my flat iron demands my hair stay moisturized.

I scrub my face, clearing it of the smeared makeup I forgot to take off before showering. That's another thing I never forget to do. Declan has my head messed up.

My phone chirps, and I fish it out of my discarded jeans.

I hope its Dec. I really hope it isn't Dec.

It's Dec.

Stop over-thinking.

I almost drop my phone; my head pops up, looking around. How did he know I was thinking about everything? I thought I played it mostly cool when I left. Yeah, right.

I don't know what you're talking about.

For some reason, texting Dec is easy. I can be myself via text. I don't feel the need to perform as much.

It's so easy to be snarky with him. Well, it's easy in real life, too, but texting makes me feel like I can really be me.

Right and I don't know what you taste like. PS It's delicious.

I take a shuddering breath, feeling my body respond to his flirty message.

Are you sexting me?

He responds in less than ten seconds.

Depends. Are you sexting me?

I laugh out loud.

Can you hear that? That's the sound of me rolling my eyes at you.

This time, I'm smiling in anticipation of his answer.

B Girl you can roll your eyes all you want. I love it when you roll your eyes. For example earlier today, your eyes rolled to the back of your goddamn head while I swallowed your cum.

Well, shit. He isn't messing around, is he?

That wasn't fair because you won't let me touch you.

I know that makes me sound like I'm pouting, but I think I kind of am. It also sounds like I'm already counting on another round. Of course I am. Naked Dec is beautiful.

I'd never been into chest hair, but for some reason it totally worked on him: his defined muscles, those tattoos, his big beautiful cock.

Without thinking, I find myself reaching with my free hand to part my robe. The cold air hits my heated, naked skin, and I hiss out in pleasure.

I didn't let you touch me bc this wasn't about me. This was about you. Besides you're not ready. When you are, believe me, I'll let you touch me all you want.

What does he mean not ready? Of course, I'm ready. Sex is the only thing I really do. The only thing I'm good for. I close my robe again; his attitude about me not being ready kills my mood.

Now tell me what you're wearing.

He can't be serious. Oh well, two can play this game.

I'm actually naked. Just showered.

Let's see what he thinks of that.

I bet your skin looks all pink and rosy. Just like your little clit did earlier before I put my mouth on it. I miss it. You should give it a little rub for me. Tell her I say hi.

And we're back folks. My phone chirps again before I can form a response.

I'm putting off showering as long as I can. I want to have your smell on me forever. Do you wanna see what you do to me?

I don't even hesitate to tell him yes. God, do I ever.

I don't wait long before my phone alerts me of a picture message. I'm not sure what I was expecting, but it wasn't a selfie of him in his bathroom mirror.

He's naked and hard. His right hand is holding his phone up to take the picture, his bottom lip is between his teeth, and his left hand is gripping his stiff cock.

It's blurred a bit, and takes me a few seconds to realize that's because it's in motion. Declan is touching himself while talking to me. Well, texting me, sexting me, whatever.

A devious thought enters my head. I've sent naked pics to guys before, but for some reason, like everything else, it feels different with Declan. Like it means more.

To hell with it, I'll do it. Before I can talk myself out of it, I open the top of my robe, lowering the collar until it's just below my nipples.

I bring my left arm under them to perk them up… I'm not exactly well endowed, and contort my right arm into an unnatural position to take the photo. I take a quick look to make sure it looks good and you can't see my face.

Once that's done, I hurry and press send before I can give myself more time to second guess my decision.

It's almost a full minute before my phone chirps, right about the time I decide I must have fucked up somehow sending him the pic.

Fuck. So fucking hot. Next time I'm coming all over your tits. Would you let me do that? Swear to fuck I'll eat you before and after. Let me come on your tits.

Everything below my waist clenches, and I rub my thighs together. I've never been this turned on from just texting. Before I can respond, my phone chirps.

Just thinking about it and I came hard for the second time today.

There's an attached picture, and it's almost the same as before, only this time Dec is looking right into the mirror and his cock is about half-mast.

There is an unmistakable puddle of cum on the bathroom counter. A puddle. I didn't think guys came that much, especially for the second time in one day.

At least, I know I'm not the only one who's being affected so strongly.

I know, in this moment, that I have to change. It scares the shit out of me.

I don't even know what I'm supposed to change into. But I know this girl won't last much longer. I know that, right now, I am the shell of a human.

I'm looking around and seeing everyone living the life I know I should be. Relationships are forming, friendships are thriving, the loyalty of Ron's group, the family they have all made. I want to be a part of that; I don't want to be on the outside anymore.

I don't know where to begin. Declan seems like the safest choice. I know he's trying. He doesn't seem to have bought into the image I present to the outside world. He's always seen through it. I know he wants to help me. I know I can't... I know it's not in me to try to love someone again, but I can be friends. I can be a friend. I can see where this goes.

S. Ferguson

Chapter 19

Bree

Sweat is pouring down my face as I'm training with Ze again. By an unspoken understanding, we found ourselves meeting every day at one in the afternoon. Today, he has me doing a lot of work using the BOSU ball: planking while balancing on it, and doing push-ups while holding the sides of it while it's upside down.

There is nothing pleasant about this but I surprise myself more than once by being able to do what he's asking.

Once again Ze waits until I'm in a vulnerable position, unable to move away, before he starts his questioning.

"So tell me about this boy." He squats beside me.

I can feel his gaze, but I don't turn my head, instead continuing to focus on raising and lowering my body while holding the wobbling BOSU. My core is screaming, and my arms are shaking, but I refuse to stop.

The physical pain is a welcome distraction from the emotional pain his question brings to the surface.

"I don't want to talk about him," I grit through my clenched teeth.

"Good thing I didn't ask you if you wanted to. I said, tell me." The authority in Ze's voice manages to come through, despite the calm tone he maintains.

I've never heard him raise his voice; something tells me he doesn't need to.

"I met him when I was 16." My mind is a flurry of memories as I try to calculate how little I can tell him while satisfying his curiosity. Realizing this is futile I decide to give him the summary, to tell him what happened when Alex left. I'm fairly certain that's what he wants to hear anyway.

"And…" God, Ze can be annoying.

"It was a year ago. I followed Alex into the store against Ron's advice. I should have listened." I pause to shake my head at my own stupidity. What else was I was supposed to do? I had searched everywhere for him. "To just stumble onto him walking into the corner store, was like a gift from heaven. I had no choice; I had to follow him. To find out what had happened to him, to us.

"'Don't go fucking searching 'til you're ready for what you'll find, Bree,' Ron had said."

I should have listened.

"I just couldn't believe that, after a year of searching, I'd finally found Alex. It didn't seem real. I was so excited. So happy and relieved that he was alive. I could still remember our last conversation: Alex telling me he loved me as he packed to go out of town for a week with his new job. I was so happy when he had found work with one of the larger construction companies in town.

We were on our way. Not bad for being on our own since we were 16. But we had each other… Always." I stare at the BOSU, refusing to look at Ze as I speak.

"I didn't know what happened to him, but I was sure we could come back from it. I was sure he had a good reason for being gone so long. We would be fine. I just needed to let him explain to me what had happened."

Then, he would wrap those long arms around me, and hold me, making everything okay again. Alex was the other half of my heart; there was nothing we couldn't get past. He was all that I had in this world, my only family, my only friend, and my lover. There was nothing I couldn't forgive.

"Then, I saw her." My face is burning with my humiliation.

She had been tall and blonde, the complete opposite of me in almost every way. She had no tattoos or piercings. She looked like someone Alex would have made fun of in the past. He always called them Mandy, Candy or Brandy, some version of a generic sorority girl name, saying their names were as unoriginal as they were. This time, however, she sauntered up to him, and wrapped her arm around his waist while placing her head on his shoulder. He wrapped an arm around her shoulders, and kissed the top of her head. The same gesture he had done with me a million times.

"Because it's the only part of you I can reach without bending in half," he had explained, when I asked him why he always kissed me there.

My heart stopped beating.

"I must have made some sort of sound because they both turned around, looking a little startled. Alex's eyes met mine, and I didn't recognize them anymore." I take a shuddering breath.

Beautiful blue eyes that held my entire world narrowed, and I saw hatred in them. The scathing look he sent me would have wounded me further had it been possible.

"'What do you want, Bree?' He acted like *I* was annoying him.

"I told him how I had been looking for him. I struggle to breathe, my heart beating out of my chest. *This can't be happening. This can't be real.* Even now the same thoughts run through my head.

"Then he fired a fatal shot. "'It's been a year, Bree. You need to let it go and move on.' Alex just rolled his eyes and turned around, dismissing me.

"I tried to explain to him how much it hurt, how he was just walking away from me. But he wouldn't listen. It hurt so fucking much." I risk a glance at Ze, he's looking at me, his face full of compassion. I don't see any pity, thank God.

"I didn't think he could get any colder after that, but I was wrong. Alex shot me an annoyed look and said 'I didn't come back to see you because it didn't bother me not to.'" At this point I'm done, I don't want to talk anymore. I also know this isn't an option with Ze.

Those words had been a cold blade slicing through my chest. Looking back, I'm pretty sure this was the exact moment my heart died. What had been left after his disappearance shattered spectacularly, all the broken pieces crashing to the scuffed up tile floor of a corner shop. I actually caught myself looking down at the floor to check if I could see them. All my anger deflated, and overwhelming grief slammed into me.

"What happened then," Ze asked, ignoring my desire to stop talking.

"Alex walked away, whispering something into the blonde's ear without sparing me a second glance. I just stood as still as a statue. I couldn't move. I couldn't speak."

I had learned in that moment that not only was I easily cast aside, I wasn't even worth a proper explanation. I wasn't worth the energy of a goodbye. My view of reality had been skewed. This was a lesson of the harshest kind. I really was the worthless cast off I had been raised to believe.

"I don't know how long I stood there. Eventually, an employee walked over whispering that I needed to leave or they would have to call the cops. I nodded silently, tears falling as I stumbled out.

"Then I walked the streets for hours, mulling over these what I had learned." I punctuate my sentence with a a tight squeeze to the edges of the BOSU.

"I couldn't talk to anyone about it. Alex had always been my best friend anyway, my only friend. I knew I needed to get my shit together. I wondered how everyone could look at me, and expect me to function, when I wasn't even whole. I had a gaping wound in my chest, blood and gore dripping on the floor. How can you ask me about anything else when I... can't... breathe?" That was the first time I'd ever spoken to someone about my panic attacks. I watched Ze's face, but saw nothing but genuine concern.

I wish I could have told Ze I eventually healed. I wish I could say I got better. But I can't. You don't recover when the most important person in your life shows you how little you mean to them, how worthless you are. Add this to the perfect storm that already was my life... No one was coming back from that.

"So that's the ending, I want to know more about the beginning. How did the two of you end up working for Ron?" Clearly Ze has no mercy for me today.

"I didn't have a good relationship with Mo...my mom. She didn't like me. She could be...cruel. Alex recognized what was going on and offered me a way out."

There, that's mostly the truth.

"So, living on the streets, that was his 'way out'?" Ze does air quotes, and gives me a look so I hard I can feel it.

"We didn't have anywhere to go. Neither of us had good parents, or access to any money. We did the best we could." I defend Alex. I don't know why, but I feel like I have to.

"If you say so… Where's your father?" Ze asks the one question I don't have to lie about to avoid answering.

"He's dead. I never knew him. Mother said he died right after I was born." The sting of all the times I spent wishing he was around makes my eyes blur with tears.

When you're helpless to escape the one parent you have, when there is no one in your corner, you can't help but imagine how different things could have been. Would my father have gone along with Mother's abuse? Would he have protected me? Taken me away and given me a real family? I'll never know, and it's pointless to keep asking myself those questions. I learned that a long time ago.

"And you're sure of that? That your old man is dead?" Ze asks, raising an eyebrow in question.

"I have no reason not to believe it. I'm 20 years old. I think I would have heard from him by now."

"If you say so," Ze repeats, giving me an odd look, like he doesn't believe it's true.

I don't know why Mother would have lied about my father being dead. She never wanted me around, so wouldn't she have wanted him to get me off her hands? It doesn't add up in my head.

Thankfully, Ze seems to think that's enough serious talk and starts directing me to move to the punching bags, which are quickly becoming my favorite part of our sessions.

* * *

Another two days of Ron-enforced time off, and I'm feeling restless. Ron insisted I take breaks before the meeting that he keeps rescheduling.

I'm beginning to think the meeting is never going to happen, and Ron is just using it as an excuse, along with taking advantage of Declan working the bar now, to make me rest.

For the first time in my life, free time isn't quite as scary. Today, I know I need to push myself a little further out of my box.

Deciding I need to act before I chicken out, again, I grab my phone and start typing a text. Friends text, right?

What are you up to?

Excellent text Bree...simple and to the point. I mentally high-five myself, and wait for him to answer.

OK, who died?

What? What does that mean? Is he joking? Maybe texting wasn't a smart choice because I can't hear his tone of voice.

Ummmmm... No one. I thought I would see what you were up to. If you're busy it's ok.

I feel like that seems desperate even if that was the opposite of what I'm going for. How the hell do you act nonchalant when you are very, very much 'chalant', or whatever the hell that word means?

I'm never too busy for you B Girl. You wanna hang out? I can bring some lunch over.

You can do this, Bree. You can do this. I take a deep breath before sending my response.

Yes.

I look around the apartment and it's still clean, but I tidy up anyway. It's never dirty…I would have to actually live here for that. I just use it to shower and sleep because it's the only place I have. This apartment isn't my home, and it hasn't been for a long, long time.

I make another quick scan before taking a quick shower, then throw on some black jeans and black tank top. I don't want to look like I tried too hard.

Maybe I should ask Ron if I could move? Before I can think any further about that idea, I hear a knock on my door.

"That was fast as hell," I say as I open the door wide for Declan to walk through.

"I was actually in the neighborhood," he responds, looking anywhere but at me.

"You were checking the bench, weren't you?" As much as it irritates me that he knows about my sacred place, I kind of like the idea that someone was looking for me.

"Maybe." He makes himself at home walking further into the apartment and sitting on my small sectional. "Lunch should be here in 10. I ordered Chinese...hope that's okay."

"I love how your idea of bringing lunch is ordering delivery while you walk here," I sass him before sitting next to him.

"So, what's up? This whole visitation initiated by B Girl has me nervous." He turns to face me and his face goes completely serious. "Are you breaking up with me? Is that was this is about?" He raises his voice a few octaves and begins flailing his arms in the air. "I knew it, you are, aren't you? You're dumping me."

I want to tell him to stop, that he's being ridiculous, but I'm laughing so hard I can't breathe. Tears are forming in my eyes as I gasp for oxygen. When I finally stop, he's staring at me. His face is serious again, but softer.

"That's the first time I've really heard you laugh. Like really laugh, not a chuckle or a smile. It's beautiful." His eyes are tender, and I find myself looking away to hide the blush tinting my cheeks.

"So, I don't have a TV. We probably should have met at your house." I change the subject, hoping he'll let it go.

"Well, we can play a game. Do you have any board games?" Declan takes my hint and lets it go.

I take a look around the apartment biting my bottom lip and

thinking hard. I know I have some cards and Monopoly, but that was always something Alex and I played together.

You can do this Bree. New life. New you. Change is good.

"I have monopoly. I know it's a long game, but we could always change the rules or something to make it go faster, if you want." I pray to God that my vulnerability isn't showing in my eyes when I ask him.

Declan's eyes are still soft when he gives me a small smile. "I've got all night, B Girl."

It doesn't take us long to get into the game and, before we know it, we're having to stop for the food delivery.

I quickly realize that Declan is super competitive. I never win, I don't expect to, but I have to admit taunting him is pretty entertaining.

After he throws yet another fit for missing the Free Parking Spot, and the subsequent $500, I can't help but tease him.

"So, I see we're a little competitive."

"If you aren't prepared to lose every friend you have while playing Monopoly, you're not prepared to play," Declan says, without skipping a beat.

We finish the game, I don't know how much time has passed, but the sun has gone down.

The kitchen light casts an almost eerie glow onto the living room floor where we're lying next to the game.

Declan won, of course.

"This was nice," Declan says. I feel sad for a moment, thinking he's leaving, but instead he rolls to his side, facing me.

I mimic his move so we're facing each other, side by side.

I clear my throat nervously before speaking. "I don't know why you enjoy hanging out, but I like it. It makes me feel… it makes me feel like I'm worth something." I'm unable to meet his eyes.

Deciding this moment is far too intimate I stand up, walking towards the living room's lamp. More light should dissolve the intimate mood. But Declan is already up behind me, stalking toward me.

"You are worth it, babe. You are so worth it," Declan moves closer and closer to me. I back up until my back hits the solid wall behind me.

It reminded me of that moment we had in the kitchen, all those weeks ago, just he and I, face to face, our breath mingling in the small space between us.

He leans into me, our bodies flush together, and I can feel every inch of him. Every single hard inch.

His hands cup my face, tilting my head to look up into his eyes. I can see desire in them, but more than that I see something else. Something I'm scared to name. His thumbs gently rub away the tears I didn't even realize were cascading down my cheeks.

"You're worth more than I could ever give you. I'll never be able to give you what you deserve, what you're worth, but I'm selfish enough to spend my life trying. I care about you enough to show you what you mean to me. Every. Single. Day." He punctuates his statement with a kiss to my forehead.

His head lowers and I close my eyes, expecting to feel his lips on mine. Instead, I feel a gentle kiss on my left cheek. "You're so strong," he whispers before he kisses my right cheek. "I know you're tired. Let me carry this burden with you. Let me in. Please, Bree." He barely whispers the last word before his mouth is on mine.

After a gentle brush of his lips against mine, he pulls away and I almost whimper at the loss, then his mouth is on mine again.

More insistent this time, his tongue traces my bottom lip, seeking entrance. An embarrassingly long moan tears from my throat when I feel his tongue slide against mine. Instead of going to its usual blank state, my mind explodes.

Emotions run through my entire body, bright colors burst behind my eyes. Need, unlike anything I have ever felt, shoots through me and, before I can even think, I grab the back of his neck and pull him closer to me.

I open wider, gladly savoring his taste as his tongue dances with mine. His hands drop to my butt, gripping me tightly and pulling up. Instinctively, I wrap my legs around his waist and feel his heavy erection pushing into me where I want it the most…where I *need* it…where I need him.

He slams my back into the wall, careful to protect my head with the back of his hand, and grinding into me.

I pull my mouth away to moan deeply, and he lowers his mouth to my neck, licking, sucking, biting.

He's probably leaving marks, but I can't find it in myself to care. Something in me craves the idea of Declan marking me…of belonging to him.

I clutch the back of his head, pulling him even closer. Suddenly, we're moving and I cling to him tightly, rubbing my chest against his, feeling his pectoral muscles push against my hardened nipples.

I can't get close enough to him; my movement becomes frantic as I writhe against him. Before I realize it, we're at my bed, and his scent surrounds me as he sets me down and takes a step back.

"Take your fucking clothes off," he growls before he all but rips his shirt over his head. I am momentarily stunned.

I've seen him shirtless before now, but never knowing I was going to get to touch him in this way. I am so touching him this time.

His chest is defined, and has a light smattering of chest hair. He's covered in tattoos, and there is a treasure trail of dark hair leading straight into his jeans.

I must have pulled his hair loose when we were kissing because it's wild and free, falling to his shoulders. He looks like a conquering warlord about to ravage his conquest. I can't help but think, *yes please.*

His chest is moving rapidly as he gives me a hard look before reaching for the fly of his jeans.

The movement snaps me out of my stupor, and I yank my shirt over my head, before toeing off my converse and unzipping my jeans. I wiggle out of them and reach for my underwear, but Declan's hands grab mine, stopping them. I look up, and he is naked, gloriously naked.

His body is long and solid muscle. His legs resemble tree trunks, and he has that V on his hips like a giant, beautiful arrow pointing to his cock. Before I can get a good look, he bends over me, but I see enough to know it's as beautiful as the rest of him.

I'm also pretty sure I saw the glint of silver on his cock. I wonder why I didn't notice that before?

"This is going to be slow. This is going to be about you, about me. This is a beginning," Declan whispers against my mouth.

I'm nothing but nerves. I've done this so many times, with so many people, but something about this moment, something about Declan, makes this feel like I've never been here before. Maybe I haven't. I take a deep shuddering breath as he lowers his mouth to mine.

His lips move against mine, and I feel his tongue slide into my mouth, tangling with mine. His hand moves to my breast, squeezing gently. He grabs my nipple with his thumb and forefinger, and pinches lightly. I gasp into his mouth, and he growls in response to the noise.

Movement catches my eye, and I realize Declan is jerking himself off again.

Everything in my lower body clenches again, as I watch his hand slowly move up and down what appears to be a fucking huge cock. It's uncut, the head showing on every down-stroke, looking red and a little angry with drops of pearly pre-cum at the slit.

I don't miss the silver hoop through the head either. I can see veins wrapped around what has to be a good nine inches, that are as thick as my wrist. There is no way in hell that thing is going to fit.

"That isn't going to fit," I blurt out before I can catch myself.

He doesn't respond, just smirks and moves so he is further on top of me.

"I can't tell you how long I've wanted this," he whispers, looking into my eyes and kissing me tenderly.

I feel tears gather in my eyes again, and I close them quickly trying to get rid of them.

"Don't hide from me, please," he says softly. I bite my bottom lip hard, and slowly open my eyes. His gaze is so full of what looks a lot like… love.

This must be what love looks like, I think to myself, reaching up and slowly cupping his cheek.

He nuzzles into my hand, and gives me another gentle kiss. "I know you deserve something more tender, but I've changed my mind. I can't do slow right now. I need this too bad. I want this too much. I promise we'll go slow next round." He leans back slightly, reaching between us.

I feel his talented fingers rubbing my clit briefly before he slowly inserts two fingers again, sliding in and out of me, scissoring them.

"Making sure it'll fit," he winks at me.

I resist the urge to roll my eyes.

Then, his hand is gone. I hear the subtle sounds of him putting a condom on. Declan moves until he is resting over me, most of his weight on his left arm as he grabs the base of his cock and guides it toward my body.

I feel the large round head of his cock pushing into me at an agonizingly slow pace.

"So fucking hot. So fucking tight," he gasps when he's about halfway in. I can feel it stretching me, a slight burn, but it's not unpleasant. Mostly, I just feel full. So full. Full of Declan… in my heart, in my head, and in my body. He's consuming me from the inside out.

He pulls out, and then pushes back in firmly, this time bottoming out inside me. We both moan as he hits my cervix.

I have heard girls before talk about this being painful but it only seems to push me closer to my orgasm. There isn't a single nerve ending, a single inch of my body he isn't touching, as he lowers his body over mine.

He is still keeping most of his weight on his forearms, but the feeling of him on top of me is intoxicating.

He slowly thrusts in and out a few times, letting me adjust to his size. He kisses me deeply, his tongue so far in my mouth and his cock so deep inside me, I can't tell where I end and he begins.

After a while, he increases the speed of his thrusts. I moan louder, wrapping my legs around his lower back, pulling him closer to me until he's slamming in and out of me, hitting some spot deep inside me that has me seeing stars.

I moan his name, clawing his back, and reach my hands down to his ass, grabbing his firm cheeks and squeezing them. Right when I'm about to come, he suddenly withdraws.

I growl my disappointment, but he just laughs and grabs my hips, rolling me onto my stomach and lifting my hips, placing a pillow under them. He releases his grip on me, and suddenly his mouth is on me. I feel his tongue lick me from my entrance to that forbidden area just above it.

My head shoots off the pillow. "What the fuck are you doing?" I shriek.

"I asked you before how you felt about ass play," I can hear his smirk, as he pulls his head from between my legs.

"Negative ghost rider," I say, trying to roll back over, but Declan's hands hold my hips, making me stay still.

"Anyone ever been in this tight little ass before?" Declan asks, moving so he is crouched over me.

I breathe out a sigh of relief he's leaving *that* entrance alone.

"No, and no one is going to," I try to say, but it comes out more as a moan as he slides back into me.

"I'll let you stick to your guns today," he says, before pulling out completely, then slamming home.

My eyes roll to the back of my head, and I give several embarrassingly loud moans. I've never been terribly vocal during sex but, for some reason, every time Declan gets his hands on me, I can't keep my mouth shut.

He moves into me over and over again, setting a steady rhythm. He raises himself a little higher on his knees, and it hits a magical spot deep inside me with his piercing.

My eyes squeeze shut and I scream, full blown scream, as fireworks burst behind my eyelids. My legs shake so much I lose my balance and fall flat on the bed.

If it weren't for the pillow he put underneath my hips, he would have slipped out of me, but the angle it creates is just enough.

Declan growls and follows me down, continuing to thrust. "Fuck, you're squeezing my dick so hard I can't hold back." He groans, and his thrusts get more and more erratic.

I feel him expand even more inside me as he finished. He moans right in my ear before sucking on the skin where my neck and shoulder meet.

"Fuck. I wanna live inside you," Declan hisses and starts thrusting again.

Apparently, he doesn't need much time to recover. He pulls out of me, placing a hand on my lower back to keep me in place.

I hear him switch out the condom and then he's back inside me, slower this time, more gentle.

"This is heaven," he says.

I don't want to believe him, but I do. I close my eyes and relish the sensation of his thickness moving in and out of me.

I don't know if this is really heaven, but for the next few hours, Declan shows me just how close to heaven on earth we can get.

Chapter 20

Bree

Something There In Between

Ze is standing in front of me, holding the focus mitts, and I'm trying my best to keep my breathing regulated.

I manage to give a mean right hook, and Ze has to put his right foot back to keep his balance. I'm pretty proud of that one.

I haven't seen Declan outside of work again, but we've been texting almost non-stop. Sometimes he gets flirty, but mostly we just talk.

It's so odd to me, a guy that isn't interested in more than just me. He doesn't ever pressure me, or demand I come over.

I did finally realize he was following me every night. I've been getting better about spending less and less time on my bench, but I don't know if I'll ever be able to skip sitting out there at night. I feel like I'm doing the best I ever have, even if the pain is still there. I'm still me; that isn't going to change. I can't undo that much damage.

Ze seems to disagree. We've given up on working out, and have been arguing for almost fifteen minutes about Alex.

"You keep acting like this guy had no choice but to leave you. I don't see it that way. I see that you're the reason you both even got off the street. Ron took *you* in, not that asshole. He just allowed him because of you," Ze says, crossing his arms in front of me.

Why is he constantly trying to prove Alex is the bad guy?

"That's ridiculous. We both worked for Ron. I was a scrawny, underage girl when I met Ron. He took a risk even letting me inside the bar, much less having me work there. I wasn't even strong enough to work for the first week," I argue.

"Of course you weren't because that boy wasn't taking proper care of you. This is a conversation you need to have with Ron. I don't know why it didn't happen when he met you, but I'm gonna tell you right now everything he did, that was for you." Ze's face is nothing but certainty.

I'm so confused. Why does this even matter now, so many years later?

Unbidden, my mind flashes back to the night I met Ron.

4 Years Ago

I was hungry, so insanely hungry. I thought I knew hunger, but nothing in my life before then could even compare to the pain in my stomach, the desperation my mind was feeling. I was getting weaker and weaker.

Alex was probably doing a little better than me; he had eaten the last of our food this morning while I was still sleeping. He had needed to because he was going out looking for work. At least, that was his explanation when I woke up disappointed and crying.

Something There In Between

He had left that morning right after I woke up, and had come back just after sunset. I was still in the same spot: a large box in an alley behind a grocery store. Part of what made this a good location was the amount of food in the dumpsters. Funny how expired food can become a commodity.

The only big issue was when the garbage and recycling trucks came on Thursdays. We had to make sure we weren't in the box when they came.

More than one fellow homeless person had told us they would just grab the boxes and smash them in the back of the truck, whether you were in them or not.

"I got you a job," Alex said, yanking me up by my arm. He looked at my face and frowned. "Couldn't you have cleaned up or something? You're gonna need to be pretty for this job."

I wanted to ask him how I was supposed to clean up when we lived in a box. I didn't even have water to drink, much less any to wash with, but I kept my mouth shut.
Alex was clearly stressed, and he didn't need me making it harder on him.

He licked his thumb and rubbed it on my face, "That's going to have to do. They said they had a place we can crash if you work out tonight."

He started walking back out of the alley toward the sidewalk, and I jogged to catch up. I was only 5'4", so I always struggled to keep up with his much taller frame.

"Hurry the fuck up!" he barked, turning corners so sharply I twisted my ankle trying to pivot fast enough.

We walked for a few more blocks, and came to an abrupt stop in front of a bar. I looked up and saw a dilapidated sign hanging above the door. It was faded and rusted out, but I think it said "Keegan's".

Before I could comment on the name of the place, or anything really, I see the symbol spray painted to the right of the door: a wolf. Everyone on the streets knows what that means: Ron.

No one knew his last name, or if he even had one. We all damn sure knew who he was.

We lived in his territory, but we didn't deal drugs. I wasn't a prostitute, and we didn't cause problems, generally keeping to ourselves, so we hadn't interacted with him at all.

Alex was walking us straight into his headquarters from what I understood.

"Wait, Alex. This place is Ron's. This isn't a good idea," I protested, grabbing his hand and trying to pull him back from the bar. I may as well have been tugging on the building itself for all the effect I have.

"Look, I don't have time for this shit, Bree. They're expecting yo—I mean us, and I'm starving and tired of sleeping in that box. I'm tired of being hungry all the damn time. This is a way for us to get what we need. It doesn't have to be forever, but if they're gonna help us, they expect something in return." His eyes look sad for a moment, but then the anger returns so quickly, I'm not even sure I saw it at all.

"Come on, we don't want to be late and risk them getting mad or changing their minds." He opens the door wide and walks in, dragging me behind him.

For once, I'm grateful for his size. I hide behind him and try to peek around his arm. I see a random collection of guys sitting around tables in chairs that have clearly been broken and glued back together a few times. I think I even see one with duct tape all over it.

Some of the guys are clearly thugs in street clothes, others are in suits. A few look like any normal guy you would pass by on the street, but I know if they're in here, there is nothing normal about them.

There is a young guy wearing a suit behind the bar, and an older man, wearing an obviously expensive suit, standing talking to him with his back to us. Even just seeing the back of his body, this man screams power, and I immediately know this is Ron. This man is going to make or break our fate tonight.

"Hey man, I brought her like I said I would," Alex says, loudly, striding toward the older man who doesn't even react to Alex talking. Alex clears his throat, and opens his mouth to speak again, but a hand wrapping around his throat cuts him off.

A guy not much older than us, with a blonde faux hawk, has his hand around Alex's neck, and he's sending him a look that I would have sworn could kill someone.

He's wearing a suit as well, but he's taken off his jacket and tie, and the first few buttons of his shirt are undone, showing off forearms covered in tattoos.

"You don't speak to Boss without permission. You stand there and wait until he's good and damn ready to talk to you. Got me?" He shoots a look at me.

"What the fuck man? She's too damn young. She's skinny as fuck, too. You been feeding her?" he asks Alex, who is starting to turn a little blue from the lack of oxygen.

Despite the other guy being smaller than Alex, he is clearly just as strong. Of course, we're in a bar full of his friends, so I know if Alex tries to fight back, he'll be dead before he gets one swing in.

"I'm 16," I say, hoping to be helpful.

I hear a frustrated groan, and realize it's from Alex, who is now looking at me like I've lost my damn mind.

"Jesus fucking Christ. Are you shitting me?" the guy asks, dropping his hand from Alex's neck.

He flexes the fingers in his hand, and shoots me a wink when he catches me looking.

Alex immediately bends over, gasping and struggling to catch his breath.

"You said you were 16?" a new voice asks, and I turn to find *him*, Ron, looking at me.

"Yes, sir," I nod and shuffle a little closer to Alex, who is still coughing but at least standing upright again.

"That changes things," he says, giving Alex a meaningful look.

"Wait," Alex starts to protest, but is cut off when Ron starts speaking again.

"The job…" He shoots Alex another meaningful look. "Isn't for someone as young as you, but I can see you need some help. Can you clean?" he asks me, and I immediately start nodding.

I would do anything for something to eat and a shower.

"You can help Greg behind the bar, keep him stocked on clean glasses, and keep the floor and shit clean tonight. If you do a good enough job, we'll make it a regular thing." He sighs; it's a deep annoyed noise. "When was the last time you ate?" He makes a point to look me in the eyes when he asks.

"Yesterday," I answer, looking at the floor. I feel heat in my cheeks, knowing all the other guys in the bar are hearing how desperate of a situation I am in.

"Quinn!" Ron yells without looking over his shoulder.

Quinn walks over to where we are standing and gives me a nod. "Yeah, Ron?" he asks, after looking at Alex like he just killed his pet dog.

"Get," he pauses. "What's your name darlin'?" Ron asks me.

"Bree," I whisper. For some reason, his endearment makes me feel like crying.

"Get Bree something to eat, but nothing heavy, because she'll get sick as shit if she's been starving all day. You," he points at Alex, "and me are going to have a conversation in my office."

Alex gulps and follows Ron as he starts walking towards a door I didn't see before to the right side of the bar. I notice the guy who choked Alex smirking and cracking his knuckles, as he follows them into the office and shuts the door.

"Come on, babe, let's feed you. You like soup?" Quinn asks me.

I can't find my voice, so I nod and follow him towards the kitchen behind the bar. Tears of hope are streaming down my face for the first time in…well, forever.

Present Day

"Where did you just go?" Ze asks me.

"I was remembering the night I met Ron. That night changed everything. If he hadn't taken us in…if he hadn't given me a place…and then Alex just left." I shudder.

"Exactly baby girl. Think long and hard about Ron, you'll realize there's something there, something in-between that you've been missing."

I take a moment and think, and, as usual, my mind wanders back to Declan, and I feel myself grinning.

I don't even notice that's the first flashback I've had that didn't cause a panic attack.

"Now, tell me why you're smiling so much more now? I like it. But I don't want to have to kill the reason." Ze's tone is teasing, but I can tell he's half serious. God knows if there was anyone who could take down someone Declan's size, it would be Ze.

I realize I'm blushing. I don't know how to explain Declan to anyone. Maybe it doesn't seem like much has happened between us on the outside, but to me, he's changing everything. I didn't know what it felt like to have someone so interested in me, just me. I don't even know how to explain this to myself.

For some reason, I find myself babbling it all out to Ze. I tell him about me and Dec hooking up. I tell him that Dec didn't push for more, that he has been texting me, and watching me like a hawk at work.

"Look, I'm happy for you baby girl. I am. But you need to make sure you're ready for this. Declan sounds like a good guy, which doesn't surprise me because I know his brother is one. That being said, it doesn't matter how perfect your knight in shining armor is. If you're not ready, it won't work. Declan can't fix you. He can't fix this for you. You are the only one who can do that. You're the designer of your own catastrophe. Don't forget that." With that, Ze walks off and I know I'm dismissed, despite not completing the workout.

Later, I'm sitting in my room running Ze's words through my head over and over again.

I know it's time. Declan has given me a glimpse of what my life could be like. I know it's probably useless, but I want it. I want to smile and laugh. I want to explore my friendship, and more, with Declan. But I know Ze's right. He's shown me how to protect myself physically, how to defend myself, but no one can defend me from me. It's time.

I dig through my junk drawer until I find the business card I'm looking for.

Amanda Walten
Trauma Therapist
520-555-7534

I make the call, and I know nothing is going to be the same now. I'm going to have to bare my soul. I'm going to have to face these demons. I just hope I'm strong enough. But I also know, for the first time since Alex, I'm not alone. I know, without even asking, that Declan is going to be there.

***

My first few sessions are rough. I practically have a panic attack during the first session.

Trying to spill my soul out to someone is hard. Amanda is patient and perseveres, letting me talk about anything or nothing at all. It doesn't take long for her to become a safe place for me.

Slowly, piece-by-piece, we deal with one broken shard of me at a time, and, let me tell you, there's a lot.

But never once do I feel shame. Never once do I feel like this is my fault.

This is a burden I've been carrying for far too long…other people's burdens to be more specific. Learning about trauma and how it affects everyone puts Alex's and even mother's behavior into perspective, and makes moving on a little bit easier.

How can you stay mad at someone when they're acting from their own pain?

More importantly, I learn about forgiveness. Sometimes, you don't forgive. Sometimes, you just refuse to let something hold you back anymore. That's not the same as forgiveness; forgiveness is for people who are sorry.

I have to learn to live and move on, despite the absence of apologies that will never come.

Sometimes, in order to move on, we have to accept that some people are just evil, and that it has nothing to do with us in the end; we just got caught in the crossfire.

I just wish I had more answers about Alex and everything he did. Amanda has helped me come to terms with the fact that day may never come, and I feel like with her and Ze's help, that might just be okay.

Chapter 21

Declan

This evening at Keegan's, I'm king of the fucking world. Bree is mine, even if she hasn't fully acknowledged it yet.

Everything has changed in the last few weeks. We haven't had sex again, but she talks to me all the time, texting even if we're not together.

She's opening her heart to me, and that is more precious than anything she could give me with her body.

Ron's big meeting, after many delays and reschedules, is finally happening tonight. Even that won't put a damper on my excellent mood.

Bree dressed up for the meeting; she's wearing her version of a little black dress, which means it's obviously black, but loose and flowing down her body to her knees. Every once in a while, she'll move in just the right way, making the dress hug her curves. In what I'm taking as a nod to yours truly, she wore it with her sparkly Converse.

If I could, I would spend my entire night just sitting and watching her. But, let's be honest, that's pretty much any time I'm around Bree.

Ron and his guys are tense tonight.

Jake pulls me aside and tells me if the shit hits the fan to just grab Bree and run out of the back door. He seems more nervous than, well, ever. Jake has always had this crazy streak in him; I don't think he was born with the same survival instincts normal people have. Jake doesn't just live on the line between fearless and reckless; he fucking tap dances on that shit.

I don't like nervous Jake. He's always a volatile guy, but nervous Jake is a whole different animal.

I especially don't like that it seems as if, when something goes down, I will be forced to choose between Bree and Jake. I can't just run out of a back door and abandon my brother.

Ron gave me a speech in his office at the beginning of my shift, basically telling me the same thing.

"Bree is your priority. The minute things look like they're going south, you grab her and you get the fuck out of here. Don't look back," he had said.

That was the moment when I knew it was officially time to start freaking the fuck out.

The most nervous person in the place tonight, however, was that Quinn guy. Hands down. Something was definitely up with him.

Quinn was more twitchy than normal, his pupils wider than normal. He kept watching Bree, too, he always did, but tonight he wasn't even paying attention to where he was walking, I saw him bump into quite a few people and even a chair once, while we all waited for the New York crew to arrive. I would have laughed my ass off at him if it wasn't kind of freaking me out.

I had asked Jake for some basic background on who was coming. He said Tony was basically the equivalent of Ron, but hadn't been quite as successful because of so many traitors in his crew.

Apparently, Tony also didn't draw the line on certain crimes like Ron did. Ron allowed drugs to be sold in his territory but if you got caught selling to kids he would end you. He allowed prostitution, but only if the women were willing and working for themselves. There were no pimps that we knew of in Ron's territory. He wasn't a good man, but he wasn't a bad man.

Tony knew Ron hadn't had the same issues, and saw the chance to ally with Ron, expand everyone's territory and at the same time get some help weeding out who kept turning on him. Apparently, he had a new second-in-command that he was anxious to introduce to Ron.

I just don't know if Tony was willing to give up what Ron was going to ask him to. Ron wouldn't tolerate that shit in any area he was responsible for.

Tony arrived with about six guys. They introduced themselves, but I barely paid attention.

To me, all these thugs were pretty interchangeable. Thugs were a dime a dozen in my opinion. Besides Jake, I wouldn't have been able to tell you the difference between Tony's guys and Ron's. Lots of suits and tattoos.

There were a few tense moments as the guys all sized each other up when they first walked in, Jake and Greg one hundred percent being the instigators of that. Fucking Jake and his inability to avoid starting shit.

Things got a little bit tenser when Ron pointed out that Tony's new second was not present. Apparently, this was some kind of insult, but Tony insisted the guy was running late and would eventually arrive.

Allegedly, his second was "finishing up some business" and had to catch a later flight. I didn't even want to think about what that business could have been.

Ron's crew aren't good guys, but I also know they aren't out robbing or killing innocents. Sure, Jake's killed, but the few I know about… Well, they deserved worse if we're being honest.

Despite all this, I couldn't wipe this fucking smile off my face. The memory of how Bree tastes, those freaking sounds she makes, and the way she feels wrapped in my arms. I reached down and discreetly adjusted the hard-on I was now sporting.

God, I couldn't wait to get out of here. I am definitely going home with her tonight. Maybe I can talk her into coming to my place? Her place is closer, but there is something about being in the place she shared with that asshole that bothers me.

Plus, she needs to get comfortable in my space. If I have any say, it'll be *our* place as soon as possible.

To say I am distracted right now is an understatement, and a huge mistake on my part.

The meeting has been going smoothly for about an hour. Tony and Ron are locked in his office, and Tony's guys are sitting around, not drinking alcohol, but at least attempting to be civil to Ron's guys in the bar's main seating area.

A few of Ron's guys have been playing pool, but no one is as relaxed as they normally are.

Greg seems to be hanging closer to Jake than normal, which is fucking saying something. Those two are inseparable.

Because of my awesome lack of observation skills tonight, I didn't notice anyone new walking into the bar.

No, it wasn't until Bree's gasp, and the sound of a glass shattering, that the new guy got my attention. I immediately moved toward Bree, who was standing just in front of the bar, still as a statue, broken glass all around her feet.

I know something is seriously wrong; she's never dropped a glass the entire time I've been here, and, in bartending, that's rare.

I take a moment to be grateful she's wearing her Converse, and not her usual thin leather flats, so her feet are protected from the glass.

Her mouth is hanging open, her eyes wide, and her expression is that of someone seeing a ghost.

"You got a lot of fucking nerve walking in here," Greg's enraged voice snaps my attention from Bree, and I look toward the stranger who has made it closer to the bar by now.

As soon as I get a good look at him, I know who he is, despite never having seen him before in my life.
Alex.

My mind is racing -- half panic, half rage -- as I push Bree away from the glass shards, and take a protective stance in front of her. She gives me no resistance; I think she's gone into shock.

Why God, why is he here now? She's finally mine. More importantly, she's finally healing. Bree is stronger now than she has been in probably her whole life, but is she strong enough to handle this?

I have a moment of pure terror: what if he's here for her?

My mind begins racing. If he is here for her, what is she going to do? Everything between us, this stronger Bree, it's all so new, so fragile.

It takes me about one more second to decide that if I kill him, this whole problem is solved.

Jake clearly has the same idea. I fucking love my brother.

He stands so quickly his chair flips backwards, and lunges forward shouting, "You're a fucking dead man."

Greg wraps a beefy arm across Jake's chest, holding him back and whispering in his ear. Jake stills, murder in his eyes, as he glares at Alex.

The moment is strangely intimate, but I file that thought away for later.

Ron stomps across the floor. I hadn't even noticed he and Tony exit his office, until he's almost chest-to-chest with Alex. He is a good few inches shorter than Alex, but I swear the taller man cowers.

"What the fuck do you want?" Ron seethes, and I swear I can see smoke coming from his ears. Bigger and taller than him or not, Ron is not to be fucked with.

Alex hesitates and looks over Ron's head towards Bree, or rather where Bree would be, if I weren't standing in front of her.

His brow furrows when he sees I'm blocking her.

Get used to it, bitch.

"No, motherfucker. You look at me, you're in my house." Ron yells, clearly at the end of his patience, and Alex's eyes immediately shift back to him.

"I came for the meeting, and I came to talk to Bree," Alex says. His voice is steady, but his eyes show he isn't nearly as calm as he wants us to think he is.

"Why, huh? You got some sort of fucking radar that lets you know she's happy? Time to come back and fuck shit all up again?" Jake shouts.

God, I love my little brother.

Greg has let him go, but is standing close. Any other time, Jake's typical smartass comment would have made me laugh, but I don't have the capacity to laugh right now.

"Meeting? Why the fuck would you be here for the meeting?" Ron looks around the room as if someone else might have the answer for this question.

"Ah, Alex, you made it. This is my second, Ron. I apologize again for his tardiness," Tony jumps in, giving Alex a welcoming look as he walks toward him, then the tense situation seems to register with him and he hesitates. Looking around the room, his gaze turns to one of scrutiny.

I'm trying to absorb what Tony just said. Alex is some sort of crime lord now? Working as Tony's second-in-command? *What the fuck?*

"Let me talk to him." Bree's soft voice comes from behind me, and I feel like my chest is going to explode.

"B Girl, no, there isn't anything he has to say that's worth listening to," I plead, turning around so we're face to face. I look down into her eyes, placing my hands on her hips, pouring every emotion I can into this look.

Please don't.

"It's okay. I'm okay," she whispers, grabbing my hand and giving it a squeeze.

All too soon, I feel the loss of her warmth as she lets go and moves around my body to where the tables are, before making her way towards Ron, Alex and Tony.

Alex immediately gets a smug look on his face. I want to see if he can still smirk when I slam his face into the nearest wall, preferably a brick one.

It disappears as someone makes an angry sound deep in his throat. It takes me a minute to realize that sound came from me.

I concentrate on attempting a Force choke. Come on, Star Wars… don't fail your most loyal fan now.

"Darlin', you don't have to do this. You say the word and he's gone," Ron says "gone" in a way that makes me think he doesn't just mean out of the bar.

For Ron to say something so aggressive in front of Tony, his men, and Alex himself, lets me know the meeting probably wasn't going that well to begin with, and that Bree is far more important to Ron than even I suspected.

Ron's voice is quiet and steady; the only reason I was able to even hear him is because I've unconsciously followed Bree's path.

Alex's eyes settle on me, and I can tell he's really seeing me for the first time. He looks me up and down, sizing me up.

I do my best impression of an angry Rottweiler, and meet his gaze head on. I'm a few inches taller, and have probably ten pounds on him.

I also know this guy is a career criminal now, which means he can probably fight better than most. I can hold my own, however I try to avoid fights when I can, which is more than you would think.

None of this matters when it comes to Bree, though. I know I will fucking kill for her. Hell itself couldn't stop me when it comes to her.

"Bree…baby. Fuck, I'm so sorry. I've missed you so much." Alex is nothing but sugary sweetness and apologetic tone, directing all his attention to Bree.

I don't miss the calculating gleam in his soulless, blue eyes, or the disbelieving snort that comes from our right. Have I told you I love Jake lately?

"Look, can we just go talk somewhere privately?" Alex says, shooting an annoyed glance in the direction of Jake and Greg.

I know from a few conversations with Jake that there is no love lost between them.

I see Ron whispering to Bree, and she whispers back. I can't hear anything they're saying clearly. I begin to walk even closer.

Everything is in slow motion, my legs moving sluggishly as I see Bree nod and take Alex's hand. He turns, and begins leading her out of the bar.

"Bree!" I shout.

She turns and looks at me, her eyes full of tears. One slowly escapes and runs down her cheek.

"Please." It's barely more than a whisper, my voice cracking, but I know she hears me.

Just like that first night I followed her to her bench, she gives me a slight shake of her head, before turning back around.

She's gone.

The only girl I've ever loved. Fuck, I should have told her. She's my reason for breathing, my soulmate. She just walked away with him.

It's only when Jake drops down beside me that I realize I've fallen to my knees.

"She…she left." I say to no one in particular, not caring that my voice cracked again.

"I know Dec, I know." Jake wraps an arm around my shoulders, resting his forehead against my temple.

And I stay like that, kneeling on the scuffed floor of a bar, surrounded by killers and the shattered pieces of my heart.

Chapter 22

Bree

Alex leads me out of the bar, away from a tense Ron and Jake. I don't dare try to think about what Declan's feeling or thinking right now. I know I'll have to talk to him about this later, but I also know I need to do this.

It's time to face my demons. Amanda taught me that. I owe her my life, and the time is now.

"Baby, I've missed you so much," Alex coos, once we're outside the large, scarred wooden doors of Keegan's.

For a horrified moment, I think he's going to try to kiss me but he must read my body language because he stops leaning towards me.

"God, you look so fucking hot. Have you been working out?" He's acting like nothing has happened. Like he didn't rip my heart out and stomp on the pieces a year ago. Like he didn't just disappear and abandon me as if I was nothing.
Something in my mind snaps.

How dare he?! How fucking dare he act like nothing has happened?!

"You know what? NO, you don't get to talk to me that way." My outburst catches even me off guard. A year of pent up hurt and anger come rushing to the forefront of my mind. There is nothing I can do to stop this avalanche.

"Do you have any fucking idea what you did to me? How long I've spent blaming myself, *hating* myself, because of your shit? You left me because you were what, tired of trying to take advantage of me and the situation I was in? I was destroyed when you left Alex. Destroyed. And when I found you?" I take a fortifying breath.

"There aren't even words to describe the pain I went through that day and every day after. But you know what, despite you, despite my mother, despite every fucked up thing that has happened to me in this life, and, believe me, it's a long list, I'm still here. I am still kicking. And I will be happy again. I *deserve* to be happy again, and it has nothing to do with anyone but me, because I'm the only person whose behavior I'm responsible for. And I'm the only one who I owe anything to. You, you're just a chicken shit who keeps running from situation to situation, abandoning ship the minute things aren't what you want them to be anymore. So, go fuck yourself. Seriously, go fuck yourself, and get the fuck out of my face. I never want to see you again." I stand back, proud of myself.

Never in my life have I gone off on someone like that. This is the first time I've ever stood up for myself. It feels better than anything else I've ever experienced. I resist the urge to wrap my arms around myself out of habit, but I know I don't need to hide from him anymore.

Alex's power over me is gone now.

Alex is clearly not expecting my tirade. His eyes are open so wide, it would be comical if the situation was better. Even I'm surprised by what I managed to say. I mentally give myself a pat on the back. A small part of me can picture Ron and Dec standing there with pride on their faces as well.

"I…I didn't know," Alex begins a lame attempt at making excuses.

"Bullshit," I cut him off. "You knew. I ran away with you. We were homeless. We fought for a life together. Then, when things finally looked up, you left. You knew damn well if it hadn't been for Ron when you abandoned me, I would have died. Hell, I almost died out on the streets when it was the two of us. I had no hope on my own. But you know what? It doesn't even matter anymore. I'm glad I got to tell you all of this, but I'm done. I never want to see you again." I manage to meet his gaze this time. His eyes look angry and confused.

I'm not that weak girl anymore. I'm not a victim anymore. He needs to realize it now, and let me move on with my life.

He makes a step towards me, and I immediately go into the protective stance Ze taught me: my feet a shoulder width apart, palms open facing him, my arms bent slightly at the elbow.

"Jesus. I'm not gonna hurt you." Alex clenches his jaw.

He takes a second look at my stance, and I see his brain working. "You've been training?" He sounds almost incredulous, like I'm not capable of learning how to properly defend myself.

"I've been doing a lot of things. Some of them good, and some of them bad, but I'm doing what I can now to get Bree back. I lost her for a while, but now I'm realizing she's not as bad as I thought, and she wasn't as far gone as I thought. I'm healing. I'm…I'm learning to be happy. I am happy." It's the first time I've said it out loud to anyone, and it feels amazing.

It feels like truth.

"I guess there really isn't anything else I can say. I wanted you back. I can get you out of Ron's pocket. I'm in good with New York. I'm Tony's Second now. I can give us the life we talked about now." His eyes lower, almost as if in defeat, as if he knows what I'm going to say before I get a chance to open my mouth.

"It's too-little too-late now, Alex." My voice is softer now. "I'm glad you're doing okay. I really am, even if I still don't really understand everything that happened with us, or between us, but that's okay. I made peace with not getting all the answers. Sometimes, life just doesn't tell us everything, and sometimes that's a mercy. I truly hope you have a really great life. I hope that everything works out for you. I just can't be a part of that anymore."

I close my eyes, and feel a tear trickle down my cheek. This is it. This is good-bye.

I'd been holding onto Alex, not really him, more the memory of him and what I had hoped he was, and from the pain that thought gave me for so long, I had convinced myself that it was actually a part of me.

Yet, as I feel another piece of my heart break off, this time I realize it really wasn't a piece of me breaking off. No, it's not pain I feel. It's relief. It's setting down a heavy burden I had been carrying for years.

This is freedom.

Then, I hear the gunshots from inside the bar.

S. Ferguson

Chapter 23

Declan

After Bree walks out the door with Alex, all hell breaks loose inside Keegan's.

The monster inside of Ron seems to spring free, and suddenly, I see why he's been so successful at the career he chose.

He lunges at Tony, grabbing him by the collar, and shaking him violently. Ron's eyes are focused, and his nostrils flaring. Someone is going to die today.

"What the fuck does he want with my daughter? I swear to God, if he hurts her, I will gut every single one of you motherfuckers!" Ron screams in Tony's face, spit flying. It's as if his anger becomes a living, breathing thing, it permeates the room. WHAT THE FUCK?

"Why the fuck did you bring that asshole in here? Was he spying for you the whole time he was here working for me?" Ron continues to fire questions at Tony, shaking him with every word. I almost feel bad for Tony. Poor guy probably couldn't answer if he wanted to, the way his head is bouncing around.

Before I can even wrap my head around that statement, Tony's guys have leapt to their feet, weapons drawn…weapons they claimed they had left at their hotel. I swear to God everything in this life is nothing but bullshit.

Jake jumps up from beside me from where I'm still kneeling on the floor, like the little bitch that I am.

Jake draws his weapon from fucking somewhere on his body, and is aiming back at Tony's guys in a matter of seconds. Greg and the others guys follow his lead. This place went from a bar to the OK Corral in 2.5 seconds.
This is about to be a bloodbath.

I know Ron and Jake's guys have the numbers, but it's unrealistic to expect that Tony's guys won't get a few shots off before they're finished off.

Just when I think this situation can't get any more fucked up, the door to the kitchen squeaks open.

"What the fuck?" a very confused Quinn asks, rubbing his face frantically and trying to take in the scene before him. His eyes are wide, and he's breathing like he just ran a marathon instead of only walking a few feet.

No one but Ron, Tony and I bother looking back at him. The other guys know better than to take their eyes off of the weapons aimed at them.

"You said you weren't going to take Ron out, man!" Quinn says, marching towards Ron and Tony. I see realization on Ron's face before Quinn continues talking. "You said the info I gave you only proved it was too risky to go through with the takeover." Quinn continues to rub his face and looks around the bar. "Where the fuck did Bree go? You said I could have her once you took Ron out."

"Shut your fucking mouth. Shut the fuck up right now," Tony growls, easing his way out of Ron's grip on his collar. I'm assuming, in his shock, Ron loosened his hold.

"The fuck? You've been giving this asshole information?" Ron's deadly focus is now aimed at Quinn. "I knew some fucker was feeding this asshole info. I just didn't know who. He came into this meeting way too fucking prepared."

Tony has the decency to look sheepish. Probably because he knows everything he's working for is now in jeopardy, and Quinn's outburst has sentenced himself to death.
In this world, there is only one way out.

Quinn's movements are so erratic. Even as he's trying to stand still in front of Ron's wrath, he really isn't. He can't keep from scratching on his arms and face. I'm amazed he hasn't broken any skin yet.

I know now, for certain, he's on something. My guess is meth. His arms move in jerky, frantic motions as he tries to explain his case to Ron, but I'm tuning him out. This has nothing to do with me.

Even if I wanted to help him, Ron's reputation for dealing with traitors is legendary.

I'm still processing the fact that Ron called Bree his daughter, and the fact that Bree left with Alex.

My world is outside of this bar right now, and I refuse to die in it. I rise to my feet slowly. I see Jake look over his shoulder at me; he gives me an unhappy look that I'm not staying down behind him. I've always been his big brother, his protector. I've never hidden from a goddamn thing in my life and that's not changing today.

Quick as lightening, Ron grabs the back of Quinn's head and forces the barrel of his gun into his mouth.

I guess he was tired of trying to listen to Quinn explain. Quinn's eyes are wide with terror. Despite my feelings about the guy, my gut clenches. We all know he isn't walking away from this.

"You betrayed me. Giving them info on me, on our crew? I knew something was up when you started using," Ron spits out, even though there is no way Quinn can answer with a mouth full of gun. He must see something in Quinn's eyes, though, so he answers an unspoken question.

"Yeah I knew you were using. Would have to be a fucking idiot to miss it, but I thought maybe you were just having a rough patch. I tried to give you a chance. That was a mistake on my part, a mistake I won't make again." He cocks his gun. "A mistake I plan to fix right fucking now." He pushes it further in Quinn's mouth, and I hear Quinn gag.

"You know what we do to traitors, Quinn." Ron's voice is icy calm. There is a second of eerie calm. Everything seems like an out of body experience, as I see Ron's finger begin to squeeze the trigger.

"NOOO!" I hear Quinn's muffled shout right before a bullet hits him in the back of his throat.

Before you can ask, no, that shit is nothing like the movies. There was fucking blood everywhere. So much splatter it looked like a Pollock painting.

The creepy way Quinn just kept standing there, swaying, a giant hole in the back of his head, for a few seconds after, made me think, *"This must be what a zombie would look like in real life."*

That's an image I know I won't forget for a long time. I've only seen one other person die before, and that image still haunts me as well.

I take back my previous statement about all hell breaking loose. This moment, right here, is when all hell breaks loose.

Ron turns his gun on Tony, who dives behind his men. The five guys are outnumbered by at least two to one, but they start firing and backing their way to the door.

The majority of their shots are wild, mostly hitting the ceiling or the back of the bar. They're trying to distract and keep Ron's men hiding under cover, so they can escape.

"STOP!" Ron roars, somehow managing to raise his voice higher than the chaos.

Miraculously, the gunfire stops. Everyone is looking around the room frantically, trying to assess the situation, and figure out who the biggest threat is.

I do a quick scan for Jake and I see he's good, having taken cover with Greg behind a flipped over table.

And me? My dumbass is still standing in the exact same spot, in the middle of the fucking room, trying to figure out how no one managed to hit the six foot five inch, two hundred thirty pound man in the middle of the room.

I'm glad they didn't, don't get me wrong, but seriously, Ron needs to take his guys to the gun range or something.

Bree chooses that exact moment to burst through the doors. Alex is hot on her heels, a gun in his hand, as he tries to grab her arm, but she shakes him off.

She runs right past Tony's guys, one of whom is bleeding badly from his stomach, straight towards me.

She runs to me.

I spend exactly one second looking at her before I throw her to the ground so hard that I'm gonna have to apologize later, and lay my entire body over her tiny one. All I can think is, *"Please God let me be thick enough to stop a bullet."*

A few more seconds go by, and I realize ceasefire is still in place.

"Tony…you know damn well me shooting this fucking traitor," he pauses to kick the side of Quinn's body so hard it slides across the floor a few inches, smearing the blood that has pooled around Quinn's head, "Isn't an attack on you. I'll give you one, and only one more chance to come back to my office. We can finish this. You and I both know if we go to war, not only am I going to win but a lot of fucking people are going to die; guys with families…innocents. But first, I need answers about what this motherfucker wanted with my daughter," Ron says giving Tony a look that I'm pretty sure could kill a lesser man on the spot before aiming it at Alex.

Alex visibly flinches before he remembers himself, and turns his face to stone.

Please take this last chance, please take it, I think over and over again.

I don't wanna know what will happen if the bullets fly again. I don't think I can be that lucky to avoid getting shot again, and I can't choose between getting Bree out of here or staying with Jake.

Some choices are truly impossible to make.

Bree gasps when Ron says daughter. I wonder if she knows he's referring to her. This is a clusterfuck.

Not to be confused with a candy bar.

Chapter 24

Bree

I hear Ron mention his daughter and I know. I just know in my soul.

He's talking about me.

I have hundreds of questions begging to come out, but I can't see anything, and can barely breathe with Declan on top of me. I know he's trying to help, but this isn't going to work.

I shove at Declan's chest, trying to get him to move.

"Not until I know they're really done shooting," he hisses at me.

"Get off me now!" I hiss right back.

I see Ron and Tony shake hands through a small space between my head and Dec's arm.

"Stand down!" Tony barks to his men, who grudgingly comply.

Jake, Greg, and the other guys hesitantly lower their weapons but don't put them back in their holsters yet. They stand, but don't flip the tables back over; they obviously want some cover readily available.

Declan gives a dramatic sigh, and then slowly rises to his feet. He pulls me up by my hands, and immediately places me behind him.

"Ron," I whisper, giving him a pleading look.

"This her?" Tony asks, looking me up and down. It's not a sleazy look, but I still don't like it. He's assessing me.

If I am really Ron's daughter, I'm not an idiot. I know that makes me a target.

"Not right now, darlin'. Let me take care of business, then I promise you, I'm all yours." Ron runs his fingers through his hair, muttering something else under his breath that I don't catch. He looks weary. I guess maybe the adrenaline rush is fading.

"That's good, because you and I need to have a fucking conversation," Declan says to me, while shooting daggers from his eyes at Alex.

"Hey, man, I'm out of this now," Alex smirks and raises his hands in mock surrender.

He walks to the area by the bar's doors where the rest of Tony's men have gathered. I guess they're not gonna risk getting far away from the door again.

"I promise, you and I will be having a conversation as soon as this is done," Ron says again, before leading Tony back into his office.

Chapter 25

Declan

I have so many different thoughts running through my head. Do I wait until Ron sorts this shit out with Bree before I tackle her with questions? Should I just grab her now, throw her over my shoulder, and run out of Keegan's? Do I take her and tie her up to keep her safe and away from this fucked up mess? Or should I wait for her to initiate things? Well, never mind on that last one. If I know Bree at all, she won't initiate shit.

"What was that?" I ask Bree, putting my hand on her lower back, and ushering her back behind the bar.

At least, if all hell breaks loose again, she can duck behind the bar. I take a moment and look for Jake. He's finally sitting in a chair next to Greg, but he's moved his chair, so his back is against the wall. He wants to make sure nothing can catch him off guard. I don't blame him.

"Alex and I needed to clear the air. It was…closure, I guess?" Bree scrunches her nose up with a thoughtful look on her face. I resist the urge to kiss the tip of her cute, little nose.

Speaking of Alex, that fucker's level of crazy must rival even Jake's. Unlike the rest of his guys, who are still huddled by the door, he's walking right into the middle of the room and taking a seat, like he doesn't have a fucking care in the world.

The arrogant look on his face shows me this move was very intentional. He wants everyone to view him as the wildcard. Too bad I don't give a fuck.

Bree looks in his direction, and gives a little chuckle, shaking her head and muttering, "He was always a crazy bastard."

She starts acting like she's just going to go back to work. I don't know why, no one is drinking right now, and no one is going to risk coming to the bar and being a lone target.

"Wait," I grab her arm gently. "I need to know what happened out there." I jerk my head to toward the doors, indicating outside.

"I said goodbye." She looks me right in the eyes as she speaks, and I see none of the pain in them I saw earlier.

"I needed to tell him how I felt. I had a lot to get off my chest. But, most importantly, I had to let him go." Her eyes glaze over when she says that, but she doesn't look sad, she looks… at peace.

I don't even think about where we are, or how fucked up this is. I just grab her and pull her into my arms.

The amazing thing is she doesn't resist. She wraps her arms around my waist, resting her head against my chest. I gently rest my cheek against the hair on top of her head and savor this moment.

I breathe in her familiar vanilla scent, and relish the calm it brings me.

"So we are…" I feel like an asshole, but I have to know.

"We are whatever we were before he walked into this bar. I don't know where this is going, Dec, but I know I'm happy. Some of it is because of you, and some of it is because of me, because I'm taking care of me. Either way, I'm happy. I want to see where this goes." She leans her head back, so her chin is resting on my chest.

"Oh, we're something, B Girl. Don't forget it, either. I'm not letting you go." I lean down and kiss her. It's a quick thing, just a gentle brush of my lips against hers.

I hear someone give a cheesy wolf whistle, and I automatically aim my middle finger in Jake's general direction, but Bree doesn't hesitate to kiss me back.

"Unless I say I'm done. Then you have to let me go," Bree says in a playful tone, once I break the kiss. I know it took courage for her to establish a boundary, and to put herself first. I like this new assertive Bree.

"You can try. I won't ever force you into anything, but I'll be everywhere you are, doing everything I can, to prove to you that I'm worth it. That we're worth it." My tone is light, but I'm deadly serious.

"Ahem." A throat clears near us, ruining our moment.

I turn my head toward the bar to see where our rude interruption is coming from. Alex. Will this fucker not go away and kick rocks or something?

"What the fuck do you want now?" I hiss, tightening my grip on Bree.

"I think I need to explain a few things to Bree. I can see now what she was trying to tell me outside. Look, I might be an asshole, but I can see she's happy. I won't try to fuck with that." He raises his hands in a surrender gesture.

He seems to be really good at that. Fucking asshole.

Bree turns to face him as well. I keep my right arm tight around her waist, half in a show of possession and half because she grounds me.
As long as she's in my arms, I know everything will be okay.

"What do you think I need to know? " Bree asks. She's playing it cool, but I can feel the tension in her body.

"I lied…about a lot really." Alex almost looks sorry, but of course, saying he lied isn't exactly a revelation.

I know this guy is a gigantic douche, and I don't know half of their history.

He takes a deep breath before continuing. "We didn't run away because of you. We ran away because of me." I can feel the shock course through Bree's body.

"I used the situation you were in, knowing your mother was abusing you. I used it because I knew you would do anything to escape, and I knew I wasn't going to make it on my own living on the streets. A beautiful, innocent, young girl is a commodity in the world we live in. I had been stealing from my parents. My dad had been threatening me with military school, or worse, with the cops. I knew I couldn't handle going to jail, or someplace where you're constantly on lockdown. You know how I feel about rules."

I don't appreciate this act, like he and Bree are good friends or something, but I can't pretend they don't have a history.

I vow then and there that, one day, she's going to be closer to me than she ever was to this fucker.
I will fill every place in her heart he ever occupied.

"Why… why did you let me think it was all my fault? Why did you constantly tell me that the only reason we were on the streets was because of me? Whenever things were rough, you were all too quick to place the blame on me," Bree says, leaning towards him and resting her hands on the bar.

I keep my hand glued to her hip. Satan himself couldn't pry me off of her at this point.

"Because I'm an asshole. Because I didn't want to accept that I was a failure. I was a punk and a thief on my best day. That's still all I really am. You were this innocent, vulnerable girl that I saw an opportunity with. Once I heard about this place, I knew that

Ron would take us in when he saw you. I didn't know he was your dad…but I thought he would be able to… have a purpose for you." Alex lowers his gaze in shame… that is if a thundercunt is capable of shame.

"You tried to sell me to Ron?" Bree's tone is all business.

"I did. He took one look at you, and I think he must have known who you were. Or it could have been your age. I kind of portrayed you as older when I had told him about you. Ron's a lot of things, we all are, but he's not in the business of selling kids for sex." Alex finally raises his gaze to meet hers.

I don't know what he sees, but he almost looks afraid for a minute.

It's kind of funny how when an abuser, whether emotional, physical or both, realizes their power is gone, they suddenly turn into chicken-shits. I saw the very same look on my own dad's face when he realized Jake wasn't his victim anymore.
He died with that look on his face.

"I don't even know how to feel about that or what to say. I'm just grateful Ron was a better man than you thought. A better man than you." Bree doesn't say it in an ugly tone, more like she's just stating a fact.

"He was. He is. Look, once this meeting is over, I'll be gone. I won't be back again; it's too risky for both Tony and I to be away. For what it's worth, I'm sorry. I was a confused and scared kid, too. I made mistakes I didn't think I could escape from. I still do. But, hey, at least I turned my criminal interests into something." Alex gives a smirk and waves his hands to draw our attention to his expensive suit.

"I can't judge you. I was young and naïve, too. I thought you hung the sun and moon, and I thought we were real. I can now see that was just a childish dream. Now, I know what love… what a relationship is supposed to feel like. I really hope you have a good life, Alex, but I'm done with you." Bree pushes herself off the bar, and walks into the kitchen.

"You come near her again, I'll fucking kill you," I growl before turning to follow Bree into the kitchen.

"You can try." Alex laughs behind me. I shoot him another angry glare before catching the kitchen door, and following Bree.

I imitate our first encounter in this very kitchen by backing her into the wall and leaning over her with both arms on the wall above her head.

Leave it to me to have a dusty, unused kitchen as the location for pivotal relationship moments.
"You love me, B Girl?" I ask, rubbing my nose against hers.

"I don't know if I love you yet… but I can definitely see it. I see how much you care about me. I see how much I care about you, but I still have work to do on me. I can't expect you to love me if I can't fully love myself. But, yeah, I can see it on the horizon. We're on our way."

I've never had someone give me such an honest answer.

And, most importantly, I've never seen Bree say something full of the one thing she's always seemed to lack: hope.

Chapter 26

Bree

Ron's meeting lasted only a few more hours before Tony and his crew took off. I spent most of the time in Declan's arms, and I had no regrets.

I noticed some of the guys, Greg in particular, giving Declan the evil eye, but I'm not worried. I don't know where this thing between us is going, but I know where I want it to go, and for the first time I have hope. Most importantly, I know that no matter what I'll be okay.

I'm strong enough now. I have the help that I need in place, and the days of tortured Bree are ending.

From the look on Ron's face when he emerges from his office, things didn't go as well as he had hoped, but nobody was shooting when they left, so I took that as a good sign.

He muttered something to the guys about another meeting being planned in a few months and then ushered me into his office.

I sent Declan a longing look before the door shut. I kind of wished he could have come with me, but I needed to face this. It was time for me to stand on my own a bit.

"I'm not good at this emotional shit, so let me tell you my side, and then you can ask me questions, okay? Just let me get this out, darlin'," Ron says with a deep sigh.

Once again, he sits in one of the big, overstuffed chairs in front of his desk rather than sitting behind it. I plop down in the chair next to his. I have no idea what he's about to say.

"Your mom and I met when we were both young. When things started taking off for me in the underworld, she didn't like it. She found out she was pregnant, and told me to quit everything and work a normal job, but I didn't have a degree like she did. I didn't have any skills. This…" he motions his hand around his office, "This is all I knew. This is what I was good at. I tried for a while, I really did, but old habits die hard, and I needed the money more than ever after you were born. I wanted to give you the world. I still do." He gives me a tender look.

"So, I started working with my old crew again and she kicked me out. At first I was angry, but I couldn't fight for you, not legally anyway. I also didn't have a girlfriend, a wife, or anyone to help take care of you, so my hands were tied. As I slowly worked my way up the ranks, I made enemies, a lot of fucking enemies, and I realized you would have only been a target for them. You would have been someone for them to hurt in order to hurt me. That's why, even when you came in here, I never intended for anyone to know." He stops to take a deep breath, his eyes looking both angry and sad.

"You have to believe me. I had no idea your mom was abusing you. I swear to you, darlin', if I had had one fucking clue that's what was happening I would have gotten you out of there. I would have fuckin' killed that bitch."

Ron's eyes are pleading with me, but all I can do is sit there staring back at him blankly. Ron is my dad. I have a dad. Then, everything he said begins processing.

"I never told you Mother hurt me," I say cautiously. No one but Alex knew that, and of course Declan, not because I told him but mainly just because he's, well, he's Declan, and he seems to know everything about me somehow.

"You didn't have to. It was written all over your face the minute you came in. For a while, I thought that fucker Alex was abusing you but I realized while he was an asshole, he wasn't that big of an asshole." Ron leans back in his chair, looking at me. "And I would have fucking gutted him."

"I always loved you. I always kept tabs on where you were, but apparently I wasn't fuckin' watching close enough, I didn't know she was a fucking heartless cunt to you. I always kept you close to my heart, darlin'." Ron waves his hand towards the painting of the little girl in his office.

I'd never really paid close attention to it before. It's always been there, a staple of his office. Now I look closely, my eyes absorbing all the details.
I gasp when I realize what I'm looking at.

That's me, probably when I was about eight or nine, at the beach on vacation. That was the only vacation mother had ever taken me on. She was forced to go to a work retreat, and didn't trust anyone to watch me, in case they found out how horribly she treated me. It had been one of the best weeks of my life. With so many people around, she was forced to be nice to me almost constantly. I had gotten to eat almost anytime I wanted, and she had actually acted like a mother on that trip.

"I know there's a lot of work to be done between me and you, but I want you to know I'm proud of you. I'm glad Alex found me even if he had no idea who I was to you. I'm so fucking grateful I got to be the one to get you off the street. Despite everything, you've turned into this beautiful, strong young woman. You're a fighter like your old man," Ron chuckles lightly.

I don't even think about it, I just launch myself into his arms. He hugs me back, squeezing gently.

"We'll figure this out, together," I say, quietly, against his shoulder.

Not too long after I finish talking with Ron, Declan informs me I'm going back to his place tonight. I don't even pretend to resist him.

I know we need this. Declan seems eerily calm for someone who just stood in the middle of a shootout, and I'm beginning to feel numb from all the emotional turmoil today caused. I know he needs this as much as I do. We need to take comfort in each other, to remind each other that we're alive, and that everything is okay.

Once we're inside Declan's apartment, he silently ushers me into his bedroom. I toe off my shoes, and pull my dress over my head letting it fall to the floor. Declan stops moving and takes a moment to stare at me. For the first time, I don't feel self-conscious, I feel powerful. I watch his nostrils flare, his pulse beating faster in his neck. He looks like he's about to devour me, and I want him to.

I walk forward, and grab the bottom of his t-shirt, some ridiculous thing with Darth Vader on it saying, "Who's your daddy?" Once his chest is bared to me, I nuzzle the dusting of dark hair before going to one of his nipples and lightly nipping it. Declan groans and grabs the back of my head, bringing my mouth to his. His tongue fills my mouth, and I suck on it, wanting to taste him.

While he's kissing me, I begin fumbling with his belt buckle, finally getting it undone, and making quick work of the fly on his jeans.

Declan breaks our kiss long enough to step back and shed his pants, pulling his boxer briefs down with them. Now it's my turn to take in his beautiful nakedness. He wraps a hand around his cock, giving it one rough stroke before ordering me to take off my bra and panties.

I comply and lay down on the bed. I don't know what he has in mind for tonight, but I know I want to see his face, and I want to feel him all around me and in me.

Declan lowers his body over mine, his cock brushing against my entrance briefly, making us both groan.

He kisses each of my nipples before kissing his way down my stomach to my core. He wastes no time thrusting a finger into me and latching his mouth onto my clit. He slides his finger in and out of my pussy, gathering extra moisture on it before he lowers it to my back entrance.

I should have known he would try for this again, but this time it doesn't bother me.

Maybe it's time to give him the one thing I haven't ever been willing to give anyone else. He already has my heart, even if I'm not fully ready to admit that yet.

"You're mine now. Every part of you. Even this." He pushes his finger fully into my ass, a little harder than before to emphasize his point before flicking my clit with his tongue as well.

"Yes," I moan. I'm beyond arguing with him, I'm beyond all thought. I am aware of nothing, but all the sensations bombarding me.

There's a little bit more of a burn when he slides a second finger in, and I spend a few minutes focusing on relaxing again. Soon, he's sliding them both in and out easily.

I feel close to coming again, and Declan must sense it, because he stops again, withdrawing his fingers and tongue.

Declan raises himself off the bed for a moment, and I hear him digging around in the dresser near the bed. He comes back in just a few seconds and I hear the sound of a cap being flicked open. Something cold slides down my crack and his fingers are back, coated in the slick liquid.

"I'm claiming that virgin ass baby. I NEED to claim that ass, B Girl. Tell me I can have it. Tell me I can take what's mine." His voice is ragged as he slides a third finger in easily, the lube making everything more slippery now.

"Take it, Dec," I moan, my head thrown back, and my words turn into a gasp.

He grabs my hips, raising me until he fits a pillow under my hips. I'm so glad he didn't try to flip me over onto my hands and knees. He puts one hand on the bed beside my head, and I feel his slick cock against my back entrance.

It feels different, and I realize he has coated the condom with extra lube.

"I want you to breathe in and out deeply, and then push back against me," he instructs me, as he carefully positions the head of his cock before starting to apply pressure.

There's a sharp burn as I follow his directions. Then, he pushes through the first ring of muscle, and we both groan. The sensation is powerful. He pushes himself in, slow and steady, until he's entirely inside me.

"Oh… fuck… Bree…." he growls my name, and I can tell his teeth are clenched from the sound. His large body is covering mine now, his hands pushing into the mattress on either side of my head.

I can practically feel him vibrating with the tension from holding back his orgasm.

"Do it." My command is breathless. I brace myself for it to hurt, but it doesn't. It's a little uncomfortable, but, as he builds up a steady rhythm, it changes. It becomes more and more pleasurable.

Part of me wonders if I could come this way. As if he's read my mind, Declan leans, creating space between our bodies, placing one hand on my hip, as the other reaches between us to strum my clit.

My eyes roll back in my head, momentarily, from the pleasure. I open them again when Declan gives a grunt of pleasure. I love his noises.

Declan's eyes catch my gaze and, for the first time ever during sex, I maintain eye contact.

I don't need to hide myself from Dec. In this moment, we are one. This is us, sharing something that is only for him and me.

"I'm close, B girl," Declan whispers, pushing himself inside me to the hilt and swiveling his hips.

The look on his face does me in, and I come apart. I shout his name, and hear him grunt again, from the pressure of my squeezing muscles.

Declan doesn't come loudly. Instead, he lowers himself so that he's completely covering my body with his again and whispers my name, like a prayer, right into my ear as he finishes inside of me.

He lays over me, supporting most of his weight on his elbows so that he doesn't crush me, and I stroke his back, just enjoying this moment. This is pure intimacy, something I've never experienced before.

"I know you said you're not there yet, but I am," Declan takes a deep breath, shivering, while I run my nails lightly down his back. "I love you, B Girl. And it's okay if you can't say that back to me yet. My love isn't conditional on you returning it. This, this was fucking beautiful, I can't wait to do it again." He thrusts his already hardening cock against me meaningfully, and I can't help but giggle.

I wrap my arms and legs around him, and put my face in the crook of his neck, just breathing him in.

Today has been a game change, a life changer. Who knew I would find my father after thinking he was dead for so long?

Who knew I would find real love, after so many years of thinking love was just an illusion?

Best of all: who knew I would find me?

Epilogue

Ron

Today started out as a shit show, and ended with me being reunited with Bree, my fucking long lost daughter.

Yeah, I'd had her around for a while now but now she knows. Now, I can really be a dad to her. You have no fucking idea the pain it caused having her so close, but not being able to show her who I was, to try to hold back from trying to fight her battles.

I tried to help her as much as I could. I gave her one of the nicest apartments I had in my shitty building, made sure she had a job, and paid her twice as much as anyone else would have, but some things even I couldn't solve for her.

She has no idea how spoiled she's about to be, now that I don't have to continue to try to hide who she is to me. I know this also means she's in danger, the same danger I spent all these years trying to protect her from, but I have a larger crew now, she's not a kid anymore, and with Ze training her, she'll be more than capable of holding her own soon, if not already. I make a mental note to get her on the gun range. I'll feel a lot better if she starts carrying.

Before leaving out of the exit from my office like I usually do, I remember I have someone to speak to.

It's probably a good idea to check the main doors and make sure they're locked and the security system is on anyway. Bree and Declan took off shortly after Bree and I had our talk. I know Bree was distracted, and Declan was all over her. Neither one of them had their heads on right.

I need to talk to Declan, too, make sure he understands the magnitude of what he's doing. I feel like he's a good guy, but that doesn't mean I won't make sure he's fully aware of what happens if he hurts my girl. I wasn't sure she would survive Alex leaving, and she showed us all what a fighter she was every damn day.

If I had had any idea that piece of shit Elizabeth, had been abusing her all those years, I would have stepped in and killed the bitch. I still might. She never reported Bree missing, so I know that cunt thinks she got away with everything. Might be time to pay her a visit.

Ze's cracked through Bree's shell, just like I thought he would, and her therapist, Amanda, has said she's making great progress as well.

Bree isn't aware I know about her therapy but when she went to Amanda initially, she couldn't afford her. Amanda had called me as Bree's employer, to see what insurance options were available for more coverage, and I just went ahead and paid most of her fees, letting Bree think she got a discounted rate. I knew Bree wouldn't just accept what she would view as a handout.

Something There In Between

God, I would give that girl the fuckin' world if she would let me. She's been the sole beneficiary of my estate since Keegan's death. Now, I don't have to wait until I'm dead to give it to her.

I walk out of my office and realize it's later than I thought. The bar is all but dark and everything's closed up.

I give a slight chuckle, as I make my way to the bar's entrance. What everyone didn't know tonight is I had a hell of a trick up my sleeve. There's a reason no one has been successful when they try to run me over.

I'm grateful we didn't need him, but I damn sure felt better he was here. I open the heavy wooden doors, and peer out into the darkness.

I keep the front of Keegan's dimly lit on purpose. I don't want it to be a flashing sign to attract non-locals and some of the…clientele… I deal with prefer anonymity and want to be hard to track.

I look around the dark street, not seeing him. Then, I feel a shiver run up my spine. He's here.

I always sense him before I can see him. There's just something otherworldly about this guy. I've never asked him about it and I never will.

I glance to my right and see a shadow coming out of more shadows. This guy might as well be a ghost for as silently as he's walking towards me.

The air around him seems to have energy. It's almost like I can see it parting to make way for him.

"Glad to see everything went well. I was a little worried about you for a minute there," he says. His blue eyes are shining despite the absence of light.

I don't know what this guy is, or who he is really, but a long time ago I helped him out of a tight spot, and he's had my back ever since.

"Me too, Casstiel, me too. Thanks for being around tonight. It helped a lot, knowing someone was here ready to save Bree if it came down to it." I reach my hand out to shake his.

"My pleasure. Family is everything. Until next time." He gives my hand a quick shake, and then slides back into the shadows as quietly as he came.

I shake my head, watching him disappear. I owe him, but that fucker creeps me out.

I turn back around and walk through the wooden doors, locking them and setting the security system.

Just as I'm walking back to my office, I hear a noise from the kitchen. I stop and all but hold my breath, hoping to hear it again.

A few minutes go by, then I hear some muffled voices, and the sounds of people moving around.

You've got to be fucking kidding me.

I slide my gun from the back of my dress pants, and slowly make my way to the kitchen door.

I'm good at being silent. Sneaking up on people is an invaluable skill in my line of work, but I know there is no way to open that kitchen door quietly. I made it loud intentionally, no one is sneaking into my bar the back way.

Once I reach the door, I know my best bet is to shove the door open and catch whoever is in there off guard. I place my hand on it, and begin to count to three in my head.

When I reach three, I shove the door open as hard as I can. It hits the wall so hard the door knob goes through the drywall.

There is nothing, and I mean absolutely nothing, that could have prepared me for what's in front of me. Not even close.

Jake and Greg are wrapped around each other, their mouths red and bruised from kissing, and Greg has his hand down Jake's pants.

They both look at me, so startled that they're frozen where they are, eyes wide.

"What the fuck?" I yell.

The End

Afterword

Something There In Between deals with a lot of heavy and very real issues. If you have or are experiencing any the issues discussed, please know you are not alone and there are people that want to help you.

If you or someone you love struggles with suicide or depression please have them call the National Suicide Prevention Lifeline at 1-800-273-8255

If you or someone you love has been a victim of sexual assault please seek help at www.rainn.org or call 800-656-HOPE

Something There In Between

Acknowledgments

The list of people I want to thank is very long and I'm still going to most likely forget someone. If I did forget you, I assure you, it wasn't intentional.

It takes a village to write a book and it has been a long journey.

First and foremost I want to thank God for always being here in between.

My husband for his unwavering support, unconditional love and patience while I wrote this book. For the many nights of coming home to a dirty house, piles of laundry and wild children because I was lost in my own world. I love you.

TH, Little Man and Oldest, for their patience, for entertaining themselves even when they didn't understand why Mommy just couldn't walk away from the computer. For showing me every day what unconditional love is, for showing me what it truly means to live, for being my redemption.

Mom for your unwavering support, always being my cheerleader even if that meant getting in my face, for tolerating the hot mess of my life, for not judging me and promising to never discuss certain parts of this book with me.

Kristine for being the other half of Team Awesome, pushing me to write, motivating me and encouraging me, for pushing me into doing author sprints and getting me to write in the first place. You may have a hug.

JD for letting me bug you with questions and bounce ideas off of you, also for naming Jake. Thank you for once telling me, before I even told you I was writing, that you could tell I was a writer. That meant the world to me. You opened up an entire world, full of amazing people, for me and I am forever grateful.

Kayla for being a great sounding board and basically saving my sanity with helpful advice and sometimes just listening.

R for being a kick ass mentor, telling me what I needed to hear even if it was uncomfortable and giving me a chance. There really aren't words to thank you properly, for everything you have done, for the help you gave this new and naive author. Most importantly you've been so kind to me, you've been my friend. I owe you my soul and then some.

Jenn for helping me more than I thought possible, for taking a chance on me, and being one of the most genuine, kindhearted people I have ever had the privilege of meeting.

Joy for being my person. I am loin deep in gratitude for your friendship. I love you b.

Julie for nagging me and being the timeline ninja, I would have been lost without you. We'll always have symbolic anal.

Thank you to Ginnie for naming Declan and to Candice for letting me use your name. Also thank you, to both of you, for being sounding boards when I started this journey.

Grant for changing my life perspective, helping me with research and being an excellent sounding board. I'm sorry I was just too awesome for Wakanda to handle.

Sierra for making me laugh, understanding my need for coffee like no other, and being a cheerleader when I needed it the most.

Sheri for being you. You never cease to make me smile, never stop being you.

Something There In Between

Leslie for being supportive and sharing your wisdom with me, your kind words have given me courage on many a dark night.

Sue for being #mamasuetotherescue more times than I can count. For taking me under your wing and talking me off the ledge and helping. You are one of the most magnificent human beings I have ever had the pleasure of meeting.

Mary for all the late night chats, the hot guy photo swapping, and for getting me in a way only a kindred spirit could.

To my BETAs: Mary and Rhonda, thank you for all of your help and feedback and unwavering support. The many messages of encouragement, all the sharing, meant more to me than I could ever tell you.

S. Ferguson

S. Ferguson is a military wife and mother of three. She loves to find beauty in the flawed and broken.

Find her on Facebook by searching her name.
Find her on Twitter @SarahFergWrites
Visit her website: www.sfergusonwrites.com
Email her at: sfergusonwrites@gmail.com

Made in the USA
Columbia, SC
20 January 2018